THE TERROR TRAP

WILLO DAVIS ROBERTS

PRESTIGE BOOKS • NEW YORK

THE TERROR TRAP

Copyright © 1971 by Willo Davis Roberts
All rights reserved
Printed in the U.S.A.

PRESTIGE BOOKS INC. • 18 EAST 41ST STREET
NEW YORK, N.Y. 10017

Chapter 1

"You want I should wait?" the cab driver asked, accepting her crumpled bills.

Cillay looked up at the house, verifying the address; yes, the number was 220, the street was Hillsdale. It was difficult to gain much of an impression, other than sheer bulk, for it was in the middle of the block and the street lights scarcely penetrated this far. However, there was a light in one of the lower floor windows . . . and they were expected, her telegram would have been delivered by now.

"No. No, thank you. We'll be staying here," she said, smiling her thanks. "Come on, Pam, we're here . . . We're at Aunt Elsa's."

Her sister roused sleepily from her own corner of the cab that had carried them from the bus station. "Cillay . . . I'm hungry."

"She'll give us something to eat, I'm sure. Come on, you can help me carry the suitcases."

They had brought only one bag apiece, as the rest of their things were being shipped on after them; they carried them easily enough, moving through the wrought iron gate which creaked as it swung inward, up the short walk to the house. It was high . . . three stories, Cillay noted, and seemed to stretch back a considerable distance from the street. The front steps were steep and well worn; there was a

5

small bulb burning in the fixture beside the door and she could see that the house was painted a dark brown.

"Cillay . . . I'm tired."

"I know, Pammy. Aunt Elsa will have a room for us . . ." She turned at the sound of the taxi moving down the street and shivered without knowing why. It was rather chilly, but not cold, and the mist made little halos around the street lights half a block away in each direction. She put out a finger and pressed the bell. She couldn't hear the sound of it ringing, which might mean either that the bell was so deep in the house that it could not be heard from here, or that it was not working at all.

The small light made a mirror of the dark glass in the upper part of the door, and she could see herself, looking lost and rather scared. Her small, oval face was framed by long, brown hair; her eyes were large and seemed more black than brown in this light. She looked more nearly Pam's age than her own nineteen years, and there was certainly nothing to be nervous about. Aunt Elsa was Daddy's own sister, for all that they'd never met her. She tried to force a smile to greet her aunt, but her lips trembled slightly.

"The case is heavy, Cillay."

She spoke quietly to her sister, automatically assuming the placid tone reserved for Pam. "Put it down, then, Pam." She wondered if she should ring again, or try knocking. Shifting her position, glancing at the windows visible from here, she noticed the sign: "Rooms for Rent". Well, of course, what was more natural than that a woman alone,

6

with such an enormous house, would rent out some of them?

She had raised her hand to try knocking when the door swung silently inward. She had heard no sound behind it and drew in a slight breath.

"Yes?" The speaker was a woman, dimly seen for the hall light was behind her: a tall, angular woman, not young, not old, with dark hair done in a tight bun in back. The voice was neither friendly nor unfriendly . . . only non-committal.

"Good evening. I'm Cillay Montand, and this is my sister, Pam. My aunt . . . Mrs. Pomeroy . . . is expecting us."

For a moment there was silence, as if this news were startling. Then, "Mrs. Pomeroy is *expecting* you?"

Cillay caught her lower lip anxiously between perfect teeth. "Well . . . yes, I think so. I sent a telegram . . . and when she wrote, three months ago, she said we were to come along here, when Mama died." She swallowed and blinked against the sting of tears. "She did . . . die, I mean, two weeks ago."

"I see." The woman spoke as if she did not see at all. She moved backward into the hallway, issuing no invitation but allowing them to enter. Cillay exhaled a small relieved sigh and shepherded Pam in ahead of her.

"Didn't my telegram come?" Not that it should matter greatly, for Aunt Elsa had said they were to come when the time arrived . . .

"Not that I know of. If you'll wait here, I'll tell Mrs. Pomeroy."

Seen under the old fashioned light fixture, the

7

woman had a sharp, hooked nose and the blackest eyes Cillay had ever encountered. She wore a sleazy rayon wrapper in a multicolor print. She vanished into the interior of the house, leaving them standing there.

"Cillay . . . I'm *so* hungry," Pam said plaintively.

Cillay swung around from her contemplation of the house . . . faded Turkish carpeting on the floor and on the stairs which rose to the upper stories, a once elegant but now faded cream colored wallpaper with gold fleur-de-lis pattern, the small stand on which stood a night light, an exquisite double globed lamp that could only be an antique . . . to look at her sister.

The face might have been a twin of her own . . . warm apricot tinted skin, wide brown eyes with heavy lashes, a sweet, responsive mouth . . . only the eyes were different. Where Cillay's sparkled with life and intelligence, Pam's were, to the perceptive observer, somewhat duller. Pam was fifteen, but her mental age was six, and the doctors had assured Mrs. Montand that she would never be any older than that.

There were footsteps on the stairs; both pairs of eyes lifted to the man descending. They saw only his legs at first; very long legs, in dark slacks, ending above well polished brown shoes. One of the roomers, no doubt? The rest of him came into sight . . . a lean waistline, a brown tweed jacket and plain brown tie, a tanned face with green eyes and a shock of dark hair, neatly combed. Not too youngish, Cillay decided . . . close to thirty, probably. But attractive. Very attractive.

She smiled at him, tentatively.

He did not return the smile but regarded them intently for a moment, then nodded. Cillay drew back to allow him passage through the hall, and he started toward the front door, then paused as if having second thoughts.

"If you're looking for a room, I'd suggest you go elsewhere," he said. And before she could think of a reply for this unexpected advice, he had disappeared out the front door.

She stared after him, bewildered, and Pam asked anxiously, "Aren't we here, Cillay? Isn't this Aunt Elsa's house?"

"Yes, darling, don't worry," she said, soothing as always with the younger girl, but uneasy within. Why had the man wanted them to go somewhere else?

She didn't have long to speculate on this, for the woman with the hooked nose reappeared, beckoning them to follow her. The hall led into the depths of the house and they followed noiselessly over the Turkish carpeting. There were closed doors on either side, and no sounds at all, but Cillay had the impression of people behind the doors.

"In here," their guide said, opening a door off a short side corridor. "This is Mrs. Pomeroy's room . . . she'll be along in a few minutes."

Again they were left alone, and without asking Pam sank onto an old fashioned settee (was that the proper word?) covered in faded green velvet. Cillay surveyed her surroundings, fascinated.

It was a combination bed-sitting room, crowded with furniture to the point where it was difficult to get around. A big carved bed, two unmatching but elegant dressers, two rocking chairs, and a dainty boudoir chair in gold and white with a peacock-blue velvet seat, a great carved chest with a jumble of items atop it, a writing desk of fine cherry put together with pegs, bookcases overflowing with books and papers. The drapes were tightly drawn, and the air was close and heavy with the odor of the room's occupant . . . faintly unpleasant, stale, old.

There seemed a mixture of valuable antiques and junk. Was the entire house packed with belongings this way?

Cillay turned eagerly at the opening of the door. Certainly her aunt must have been anticipating their arrival; it didn't matter that this strange woman had not known of them.

Somehow she had unconsciously assumed that Elsa Pomeroy would resemble her father, whose older sister she was. The woman who entered now was nothing like the tall, gentle-faced man Edward Montand had been. She was short (shorter than Cillay who wore junior petite dresses) but very fat . . . she must have weighed close to two hundred pounds, for the flesh rolled over the edge of her collar and trembled in a gelatinous manner on her arms which strained the sleeves of her dress. Her hair was an unlikely black, drawn back into a knot somewhat untidily. Only her eyes might have been considered to be a Montand heritage, for they were almost as dark a brown as Cillay's own.

She advanced upon the girls, threading her way through the clutter without looking at it, the dark eyes missing nothing.

10

"Aunt Elsa?" Cillay asked hesitantly, her smile wavering when there was no smile in return.

The woman's voice was husky, as if she had a cold or smoked too much. "Which one are you?"

"I'm Cillay." She pronounced it carefully, the accent on the last syllable, for it was often mispronounced by those who saw it written. "And this is my sister, Pam. Aunt Elsa, didn't you get my telegram, saying we were coming?"

"No. Western Union's snarled it up some way, no doubt. Take your money, but don't hurry to deliver your messages. As bad as the post office, these days."

"But it's all right that we came, isn't it?" Cillay met the other pair of eyes with some anxiety. "I mean," she fumbled in her bag for the letter, "you wrote Mama that we could come."

She brought out the letter, addressed in a spidery hand to Mrs. Dorothy Montand, Box 17, Serling, Illinois. "You remember answering her letter to you?"

"Yes, of course, I'm not senile yet. Only I didn't get any telegram, so it's a bit of a surprise. Let's see, your mother wrote . . . how long ago was it?"

"About three months ago. When she found out . . ." Cillay choked over the words, "that there was nothing the doctors could do for her. You're the only relative we have left, now that she's gone . . . and when you told her you would leave your property to me one day . . . you can't imagine what a relief that was! Because I have to look after Pam, you see . . ."

The hook nosed woman had come to the doorway behind Elsa Pomeroy. She was staring at Pam, who had nearly fallen asleep on the velvet settee.

11

"What's the matter with her? Doesn't she talk for herself at all?"

"Oh, yes, she speaks. But she's a child, you see . . . the doctors said she'll never be any older, mentally, than she is now. Mama was so afraid they'd put her into a home or something . . . she made me promise not to let them do that. But it won't be necessary now, will it, so long as we can stay here with you."

The two women exchanged a message with their eyes; their faces revealed nothing of its nature, and Cillay felt a moment of uneasiness. But Elsa spoke matter-of-factly.

"Don't you worry about a thing. If I said I'd take you in, you may be sure of it. Beatrice, what do we have in the way of empty rooms? Nothing on the first floor, I think. The third back on the second floor?"

"Sharing a bath with Mr. Chellmand?" Beatrice displayed mild shock. "I wouldn't think that would do, Pet."

"No. No, you're right. Then it'll have to be the third floor, I'm afraid . . . although you've got young legs, it won't bother you. The two small rooms in the back are made up, aren't they? That way they wouldn't have to share a bath with any of the roomers."

Beatrice nodded. "All right. Shall I take them up now, then?"

"Please," Cillay asked uncertainly, for this was hardly the welcome she had anticipated. "I wonder if we might have . . . have a bite to eat, before we go up, if it wouldn't be too much trouble? My sister is

12

very hungry . . . the bus didn't stop anywhere long enough to get a real meal today."

"Of course. Get them something, Beatrice. I've got to get back to the television . . . there's a special on in ten minutes. You might bring me a snack, too, when you get around to it."

"All right. Come this way," Beatrice said, and led the way out of the room.

They passed a large dining room, where places . . . she couldn't count quickly enough to determine how many, but surely eight or ten . . . were already set out for breakfast. The kitchen was down a short corridor, around a corner, and down three steps, a big room that was rather gloomy under the dim lights. Everything here was old fashioned, too . . . there was a gas stove that was surely far older than Cillay, one with eight burners instead of the usual four. A table and chairs, two refrigerators, a chest freezer. The linoleum was worn and even dangerous in places; it needed replacing rather badly, which was surprising. Cillay's impression from the letter she carried in her purse was that Elsa Pomeroy was fairly well-to-do.

"Sit down. I'll get you something," Beatrice said. She seemed to have the knack of being neither gracious nor rude, but somewhere in between. Not interested, Cillay thought. She doesn't care about us, one way or the other.

"Do you . . . work for my aunt?" she asked, settling Pam in one of the chairs at the table.

"I assist her," Beatrice said in that flat manner she had. She moved from counter to refrigerator, bringing out milk and bread and cheese and a bowl of fruit.

"Are there many roomers here now?"

"Six," was the answer. "We have only one room left on the second floor. The third floor rooms are harder to rent . . . people don't like climbing stairs."

But we have strong young legs, Cillay reminded herself. What's an extra flight of stairs?

She made sandwiches for herself and Pam. Beatrice poured out tall glasses of milk for them. Cillay hadn't been hungry until she began to eat; then, suddenly, she was ravenous. She'd been too nervous to develop an appetite before, perhaps.

"One of the roomers came down while we were in the front hall," Cillay said, feeling a compulsion to make conversation with this woman, to break through her reserve. "A tall man with dark hair, very nicely dressed. Which one would that be?"

"Mr. Chellmand, I expect. He's on the second floor. When you're finished I'll take you up to your rooms."

That seemed to be a hint that she might better concentrate on eating rather than talking, and Cillay subsided to eat her way through a second sandwich and a banana. Pam was nearly falling asleep on the table, and it was, indeed, time to get her to a bed.

For all her young legs, Cillay was tired by the time they reached the third floor. There were two sets of stairs, Beatrice informed her; the ones Mr. Chellmand had used in the front, and a second set which rose from the back of the house. It was these which they climbed, narrow and making several

14

turns, so that Cillay lost her sense of direction before they reached the top.

"It's confusing, isn't it? It's such a large house."

"They built several additions onto the original," Beatrice admitted. "But I don't think you can actually get lost. Here, you can take this room, and there's a bath in between, and then the room for your sister. Everything's old fashioned . . . we haven't done much modernizing on this floor as yet. Not worth it unless we put in an elevator, and that's too expensive . . . most of our roomers are older people, and they can't get up two flights of stairs."

"I noticed the table was set. Will I meet them in the morning? Does everyone eat together?"

"Most of them. Breakfast is at eight." Beatrice moved ahead of them, turning on lights, none of them over sixty watts. "I think you have everything now."

"Yes. Thank you very much." Cillay tried to put warmth, genuine appreciation, into her voice, but Beatrice remained unmoved. It was, in a way, a relief when they were left alone.

Pam stood in the middle of the second bedroom, her eyelids drooping. "I'm tired," she said.

It took only minutes to locate her nightgown in the suitcase and turn down the bed while her sister undressed. The room was small and the furniture all looked as if it had been installed when the house was built, perhaps about 1900, but it was clean and the mattress seemed firm and without lumps. Pam was asleep before Cillay had drawn the blankets up over her.

She was, herself, feeling suddenly and overwhelmingly sleepy. It was almost as if she had been drugged . . .

She laughed at her own fancies, deciding that it was impossible to stay awake long enough to take a bath. It had been a long journey, made more tiring by the emotional climate of having recently lost her mother and the uncertainties of the future. Aunt Elsa seemed a strange woman . . . not at all what she had imagined . . . but she had taken them in as promised . . .

She realized she was dozing, and she had not yet turned out the light. She stretched her fingers toward the lamp at her bedside and couldn't have said whether or not she turned the switch before the languor of sleep overtook her.

When she awoke some hours later the room was in total darkness and she did not know, for a moment, where she was. But she was sure there was someone in the room with her, for she heard the controlled breathing. Not Pam. Pam would have called out her name, probably without getting out of her own bed. Cillay floated in a semi-conscious state, trying to drag herself out of the depths of sleep.

Before she could accomplish this, she heard the creak of the door, and then the gentle click as the lock engaged. She sank back into the euphoric state of nothingness and was unaware of the faint protesting sounds made by the stairs as the intruder crept silently down them.

Chapter 2

She woke feeling thick headed, dry mouthed. She rolled over in alarm, for the sun was streaming in the single window. Her watch . . . the one valuable Mama had possessed, which had been given to Cillay before her death . . . showed the time to be five past eight, and Beatrice had said breakfast was at eight.

The knowledge that she was already late brought her out of bed, staggering somewhat, to hurry through the bathroom to call her sister.

Pam was already up and was dressing in a blouse and plaid jumper. She turned her sunny smile in Cillay's direction. "I'm hungry, aren't you? I hope we can have eggs for breakfast. Do you think Aunt Elsa will let us have eggs?"

"I don't know, but we're late, so hurry. It'll be ready in a minute, and we'll go down."

She dressed as hurriedly as she could, but it was difficult to find everything in the suitcase, and she had to take time to wash her face with cold water . . . it was all that came out of the taps, although undoubtedly if she let it run long enough it would have warmed . . . so that by the time they reached the first floor it was nearly eight-thirty.

Aunt Elsa was still at the table, but Beatrice had apparently finished for she was doing something in the kitchen. Cillay cast a quick glance around the board, hoping to see Mr. Chellmand of the inexplicable remark, but he was not there. Instead, there were three elderly ladies and an elderly man, all of them masticating toast with their false teeth and sipping at steaming coffee.

"I'm sorry," Cillay said breathlessly. "We slept too late . . . I guess we were more tired than we realized, last night."

Aunt Elsa nodded. "Traveling is very tiring. Buses are dreadful. I can't think why anyone rides them." Cillay might have told her that the main reason was that they were cheaper than other modes of transportation, but Elsa didn't give her a chance. "Sit down . . . there, and there. There are scrambled eggs this morning . . . Beatrice will bring them in. You may start with toast and coffee, if you like."

There was also a glass of tomato juice at each place. Cillay reached for hers eagerly, for the dryness of her mouth persisted; it was a disappointment to find that the juice was unchilled, but she drank it anyway.

"This is my niece, Cillay Montand," Elsa said, her eyes sweeping the table. "And her sister, Pam." She went on to introduce them all.

Mrs. Sanding looked to be in her early seventies, a tiny lady with snowy hair and bright blue eyes which peered out at them through bifocals. She smiled at them in an alert manner, as she had toast in her mouth and could not speak.

Next to her was Miss Appleton, who looked to be somewhat older; she had a round, cherubic face and was wearing one of the new shades of pale lipstick and just a touch . . . good grief, was she actually wearing faint blue eyeshadow? She, too, bobbed her head pleasantly, and Cillay drew her eyes away, with an effort, from Miss Appleton's hair, which was a lovely but hardly natural shade of pale blue.

Next in order around the table was Mr. Gary, whose first name was Adam, and he was on a first name basis with them all. Mr. Gary informed her, in a chummy fashion, that he was seventy-six, but she needn't think he was a doddering old codger, for he had quite a bit of life in him yet; all the old ladies snickered appreciatively at this. He was thin and wrinkled and his white hair was sparse, but he did, indeed, appear to be quite spry in his movements.

The final member of the breakfasting group was Mrs. Fontana, slightly younger than the others . . . perhaps in her middle sixties. She seemed a mild, quiet little person with no visible peculiarities.

Beatrice brought in, silently, two plates of scrambled eggs. She had gotten them too dry, but Cillay was hungry enough not to mind, and Pam docilely picked up her fork and made her way through them. This was a relief as Pam, while never knowingly rude, sometimes had the childish habit of expressing her likes and dislikes all too truthfully.

The old people had finished before the girls, and excused themselves. Aunt Elsa remained at the table, regarding them speculatively.

"We have got to decide what to do with you . . . to occupy your time, I mean. I suppose your sister doesn't go to school?"

"No. She can do simple things . . . peel potatoes, and dust, things like that. She likes to draw. She's

19

quite good at it. She doesn't get into trouble or anything like that."

"And you . . . you've finished school?"

"I had one year of junior college, before . . . before Mama died. I had intended to go back this year, but there was no one to stay with in Serling, and very little money." She didn't mention that she had had few friends any more, for the past year Mama had grown more and more ill, and all the time not devoted to classes had been spent in caring for her and Pam, so that there was no time for friends. "I had thought about getting a job . . . I type a little . . . but there was no one to leave Pam with. She doesn't deliberately do anything she shouldn't, but she can't really be left all alone, any more than you could leave a small child."

"Well, there's plenty to do around here. Great barn of a house, and it's usually full of roomers. Most of them eat here, too, so . . . I don't suppose you can cook?" Elsa fixed sharp dark eyes on her, hopefully.

"Yes, I can do most things. I did all the cooking when Mama was . . . sick."

"Beatrice is a miserable cook. We shall have to let you try your wings there. Is your sister up to washing dishes?"

"Well, she tends to sort of . . . you know, play in the suds. But she wipes efficiently."

Elsa Pomeroy grunted. "We'll find tasks for both of you, I should think. Enough for you to earn your keep, all right. Bring your dishes to the kitchen when you've finished eating, and Beatrice will tell you what to do then."

20

Cillay stared after her, somewhat unsettled. She had expected to pitch in and help, of course, but after the cordial invitation her aunt had issued in response to her mother's plea only a few months ago it seemed odd to be told that she would have to earn her keep.

She resolved to reread the letter when she went back upstairs to see if they had all somehow misinterpreted the attitude of it.

But it was some time before she got back to her room. Beatrice had all sorts of ideas on what they could do, which included starting with the breakfast dishes. She saw, when she began to work in the kitchen, that everything was less than clean . . . certainly not up to the standards her mother had demanded. A greasy film over the stove, surely left there for several days, yielded to cleanser and a rag; she put Pam to work scrubbing the floor, which the girl did well if slowly. It was, Cillay discovered when she finally hung up the last of the cleaning rags, nearly eleven o'clock.

She found her aunt in a back parlor, sucking the insides from a chocolate and watching a new and expensive looking color television.

Elsa Pomeroy looked up at her with a smile. "All done? Like to watch soap operas? No? Just as well, they're habit forming, and there isn't time to do any work if you waste so much time, is there? Most of the ladies are in the front parlor, I think, if you want company."

Company. Those old ladies and an old man. Cillay withdrew from the room, made queasy by the sight of the fat woman sucking at her chocolates, and wondered how she would ever get acquainted with any young people in this strange city. It looked as if Aunt Elsa intended to keep her rather busy with housework, and there were no young people in this house. Except that Mr. Chellmand, who could certainly not be classified with the others.

They wandered into the front parlor, and Pam was immediately taken by a magazine with brightly colored pictures. She settled down to look through it, where she should be safe for half an hour or so.

Mrs. Sanding, the tiny one with glasses, looked up at her expectantly. "I don't suppose you play bridge, do you, young lady?"

"No, I'm afraid not," Cillay confessed.

The old lady sighed. "Elizabeth plays, Miss Appleton, you know, and Mr. Gary. But we can't get up a fourth . . . Emily . . ." she cast an exasperated glance at the innocuous Mrs. Fontana, "won't even try to learn."

Mrs. Fontana smiled weakly. "One has to have the brain for bridge, doesn't one? And I'm afraid I don't remember the cards well enough. It's not my age, you know, it's simply that I never had that sort of brain."

Mrs. Sanding muttered something that sounded suspiciously like, "nor any sort of brain," but Mrs. Fontana went on smiling so she couldn't have heard. She was knitting something soft and pink, and she paused to attach a new length of yarn.

Cillay moved to the window, looking out into the street that had seemed almost threatening last night. Today, in the sunshine, it was an ordinary street of old buildings, most of them now turned into apartments or rooming houses. There was, she discovered, a tiny plot of lawn in front of this house, and Miss Appleton was out there, loosening the soil around a row of chrysanthemums while Mr. Gary stood by to give her advice. The old lady's blue hair was even more startling out in the bright sunlight.

Mrs. Sanding moved to stand beside her. "Pathetic, isn't she?"

"Pathetic?" Cillay echoed. She would have said, rather, that the old girl was making a valiant effort to hold back the years.

"Making a play for Adam Gary that way. She follows him around and asks him, 'What do you think, Adam?' about everything from the weather to how the soup is. And it's always frightful in this place, believe me. It's disgusting, at her age. She's much too old for him."

Startled, Cillay said nothing. This, she found, did not deter Mrs. Sanding from continuing.

"She's eighty years old! Well preserved, I'll admit, but good heavens! Adam is only seventy-six!"

Again Cillay could find no reply, although she was beginning to be intrigued by this group. Was Miss Appleton seriously "making a play" for Mr. Gary?

"I'm seventy-two, you know," confessed Mrs. Sanding. "I think a man likes a woman to be a few years younger than himself, don't you think so?"

"Do you really think a few years matter, one way or the other, when one reaches our ages?" Mrs. Fontana asked gently.

"Well, eighty! Good heavens! You know something?" Mrs. Sanding leaned closer to Cillay with the air of one about to reveal a delightfully wicked secret. "It's a wig! That blue hair is a wig! She's practically as bald as an ostrich egg! She doesn't know it, but I saw her, once, without it! Bald as an ostrich egg!"

"Is that right?"

Mrs. Sanding nodded vigorously, as if it were to her credit that *she* didn't need a wig. She heaved a sigh. "Well, if I can't get up a bridge game I guess I'll look through that magazine that had the good recipes. Maybe Beatrice could be persuaded to try one of them, although I doubt it."

Cillay, left to herself, saw that Pam was still absorbed in the colored pictures. A breath of air would be nice, she thought, and paused beside her sister's chair. "I'm going out for a few minutes. Will you stay right here in this room until I come back?"

Pam nodded without taking her eyes off the pages. Mrs. Sanding turned to fix a moderately suspicious eye on the younger girl.

"She's not dangerous, is she?"

"Oh, no, please don't think that! She's . . . she's a very sweet little girl, and she'd never hurt anyone or anything!"

"Oh. Well, we'll keep an eye on her, then," Mrs. Sanding offered. "You go have your walk; I don't doubt you've earned it."

She spoke briefly to Miss Appleton and Mr. Gary in the front yard, and moved through the iron gate hearing the old lady saying, "I like the dark golden ones the best, don't you? Or do you think these would look better on the table, Mr. Gary?"

Cillay smiled, never having realized that romance

24

was still a part of life at seventy and eighty, somehow pleased at the idea.

"It might be that long before any romance comes into my life," she said aloud, but she didn't believe it. On a lovely autumn day, when a girl was nineteen and reasonably pretty . . . she hadn't been around young men enough in the past year to have heard that she was more than that . . . anything exciting could happen.

She didn't walk far down the street, because she was afraid of getting lost. There were many little side streets, odd joggings and turnings, and in at least one instance she realized that the street signs had been turned a quarter turn so that names were credited to the wrong streets. It wouldn't do to become confused and be late to lunch, as well as breakfast, on her first day!

As she turned in the gateway at number 220, a young man came bursting out the door and down the steps, almost running into her. He stopped short, looking in amazement.

Cillay looked, too. Not much older than herself, she thought, with a pleasant face, fair hair and gray eyes, rather stocky but moving with the ease of an athlete. He wore jeans and a sweat shirt that said City University across the front of it.

They stepped, each of them, politely to one side. The same side. Immediately they each took a step in the opposite direction, and the boy began to laugh.

"Sorry. I haven't got time to waltz properly with you, though I'd love to. Do you live around here?"

Cillay gestured at the house behind him. "I've come to stay with my aunt."

25

"Your aunt?" He sent a startled glance backward, then brought his eyes back to her face. "Your aunt lives here?"

"Yes. Mrs. Pomeroy."

Something flickered in his eyes and was gone. Or perhaps she had imagined it, for he was smiling again now.

"That's great! I live here, too, my name's Alan Creighton, but I'm late for a class and I have to run . . . I'll see you tonight!"

She turned to watch his progress . . . He was running, not looking back . . . and smiled. So there was another young person in the house; she was enormously cheered by that.

She found Pam waiting patiently for her, magazine closed in her lap, small face upturned. "Can we go upstairs, Cillay? I'm cold; I'd like a sweater."

"All right. Come along. We'll go up the front stairs this time, shall we, and learn our way around?"

They paused on the second floor landing to peer down the long corridor which bisected that story. There were many doors, all of them closed, none of them disclosing any secrets. But there were secrets behind them, Cillay thought, intrigued. Each of them held whatever these people had accumulated during a lifetime. It would be fun learning about them. She didn't add "especially Mr. Chellmand and that Alan Creightor," but her steps were lighter, climbing the remaining stairs.

Their beds were unmade, because of their hasty descent for breakfast, and they had not yet unpacked their clothes. Cillay quickly did this, hoping that the rest of their clothes would be along before they ran

26

out of things; she must ask Aunt Elsa about washing facilities.

Only then did she remember that she had intended to reread Aunt Elsa's letter; she couldn't reconcile it with what she had seen of her aunt in person. She had tucked it back into her purse, and the purse had sat where she dropped it upon entering the room last night, on a chair just inside the door.

Incredulous at first, but convinced by dumping the contents of the bag out onto the bed, Cillay stared thoughtfully down at her meagre belongings.

The letter was gone.

Chapter 3

There wasn't time to think too much about it. Lunch was served at twelve-thirty, and she was requested to carry in the soup.

Mrs. Sanding's evaluation of the soup proved accurate: it was too watery, had too much cabbage, and nothing for seasoning except salt, and not enough of that. It was served with crackers and followed by bowls of equally watery custard. Pam looked up from hers and said brightly, "It's not as good as yours, Cillay."

"Then for heaven's sake let Cillay make it next time," Mrs. Sanding piped.

Elsa Pomeroy poked at her own portion. "It's not particularly palatable, Beatrice. You did something wrong."

Beatrice was frozen faced. "You can't expect me to cook and do everything else in this house as well at the same time," she said coldly.

As Cillay and Pam had totally taken over the cleaning of the kitchen that morning, she felt they deserved some credit for part of that activity, but Cillay said nothing, her cheeks faintly pink in embarrassment at what Pam had innocently started.

Mrs. Pomeroy pushed her dish away, half eaten "I believe I'll have a couple of chocolates, instead. Maybe you'd get them from my bedroom, child . . . you've younger legs than I have."

Cillay moved obediently after the chocolates. There was an opened box on the desk in her aunt's room. She couldn't help noticing the clutter of papers and envelopes protruding from the pigeon holes and there, lying on the surface of the desk itself, was surely her mother's own letter to Elsa. The letter telling her sister-in-law that she was dying, leaving two homeless girls, and asking her for help.

She had had it out, then, since the girls had come. She'd reread what Dorothy Montand had written. As Cillay had wanted to reread Elsa's reply. What had happened to that letter? She distinctly remembered having started to pull it out of her purse while she was in this room last night, and then replacing it.

A vague impression drifted into her mind as she picked up the box of candy, the impression of extremely deep sleep, of a presence in her room, of the sound of the bedroom door closing quietly.

A dream. Surely no more than a dream. Cillay laughed at herself, making her way back to the dining room. The next thing she'd be imagining that Beatrice had slipped something into that milk she'd given them last night, something to make them sleep (as if they'd needed anything, after that lengthy journey!) and then sneaked back upstairs to steal her letter! For why should anyone have wanted to steal it? Beatrice worked for Elsa, and Elsa certainly knew what was in her own letter, didn't she? The letter must have fallen out of her purse, unnoticed; it was certainly not important.

Mrs. Pomeroy chose, with great care, one of the chocolates; she made no move to offer them around, and, actually, Cillay felt a sense of repugnance at the

29

way her aunt ate them . . . biting through the outer layer of chocolate as if it were an eggshell and then noisily extracting the soft center . . . that killed any desire she might have had for one.

Pam raised her head, the large dark eyes seeming almost glazed, and said softly, "I'm sleepy, Cillay. I think I would like to take a nap."

"Yes, of course. Come on, I'll take you up," Cillay said, glad of an excuse to leave the table herself without finishing the dreadful custard. She was, however, still somewhat hungry, and as the kitchen was empty when they passed through it she picked up two apples from the bowl on the table and took them along.

Pam fell asleep almost instantly, the way she usually did. But Cillay, alone in her own small room, felt no inclination for a nap. The apple was crisp and sweet and she ate it, pacing the worn rug, thinking. She was not tired; last night's sound sleep had taken care of the strain of the trip from Illinois. She felt young, and vital, and alive . . . and she wanted to do something interesting, but she didn't know what there was to do.

In the end, wiping the apple juice off her mouth and replacing her pale lipstick, she made her way back downstairs and was caught up in the cleaning again. There was not so much to do, this time, for she had taken care of most of the extra work that morning. Beatrice stayed in the kitchen, helping, and once Cillay caught an expression on her face that was alarming . . . why, it was almost as if she hated the younger girl, and there was no justification for that.

The afternoon stretched ahead, wonderfully free. She was wary of wandering far from the house . . . perhaps that nice Alan Creighton would help her learn her way about the immediate neighborhood . . . and she hadn't spotted anything particularly desirable to read . . . considering Beatrice's ineptitude in the kitchen, maybe it would be a good idea to bake something.

Her aunt looked up in wonder when she put her request. "You know how to bake bread?"

"Yes. I used to make it often for Mama. If there's yeast in the house . . ."

"There used to be some, if it's not too old. Go ahead, cook something. If you can do better than Beatrice, maybe I'll replace her."

Was that why the other woman had given her such a malevolent look? Was she jealous of Cillay? Did she fear for her own position in this house? It was a relief to have thought of a reasonable explanation, and Cillay resolved to do nothing to antagonize Beatrice.

She liked making bread, kneading the springy dough, forming the loaves and setting them to rise. The kitchen was cool for that; perhaps she could also make a batch of cookies, and the heat from the oven would expedite the rising of the bread. She hummed as she worked, feeling that if she could make a place for herself here . . . not taking anything from Beatrice, but making herself needed and appreciated . . . she could indeed pay her own way and Pam's; perhaps her aunt would be willing to pay her a small salary in addition to her room and board, for her own supply of money was small and

31

there would eventually be expenses to be met . . . Pam would need shoes before long, for instance, and she herself did not possess a warm winter coat.

The cookies came out of the oven, crisp and fragrant; she spread them out on the table to cool, and while the bread was baking she sat on the back steps to enjoy the late afternoon sunshine.

There was actually little yard space, for although the lot was a large one the house took up nearly all of it. Cillay prowled around a little, looking into the ancient two car garage with its dirt floor and nothing to suggest it had ever had a car in it. There was a tool shed, filled with shovels and pry bars and such. On each side of the lot was a high board fence, effectively blocking off any view of the neighbors, and eliminating any chance to get acquainted with them.

There were hundreds of thousands of people in this city, and she didn't know any of them. It was an awesome thought, and she shivered a little. But of course that boy . . . Alan Creighton . . . lived in one of those rooms on the second floor, and he had indicated his willingness to be friends. She wondered if he would be returning soon, and thought that she might better be sitting on the front steps, but she could not until her bread came out of the oven.

She had made six loaves, and they rose to golden-crusted perfection. Beatrice, who had come into the kitchen to check on dinner preparations, eyed it without comment, but the rest of the household was not so complacent.

"What's that you're cooking back there?" Mrs. Sanding demanded when Cillay met her in the hall. "The odors have been tantalizing us all afternoon!"

32

"Only thing I don't care for about this place," old Mr. Gary admitted . . . "the food, you know. They seem to think because we're all past the first flush of youth we're satisfied with pap, but I've got a three hundred dollar pair of teeth that guarantees I could chew a steak . . . could I get hold of one."

"I can't imagine," quiet little Mrs. Fontana said in her soft voice, "why one would hire out to cook if one had no ability at all in that direction. Can you?"

"I thought maybe Beatrice was related to Mrs. Pomeroy," Miss Appleton observed; she had come in from outside and took off her wide brimmed hat, hanging it on the mahogany tree in the front hall; "Is that the case, Miss Montand? Or do you mind if I call you Cillay, as you're so much younger than I am?"

"That's no exaggeration," Mrs. Sanding muttered in that way she had, which everyone seemed to ignore although Cillay found it quite easy to understand what she said in these asides.

"I don't think she's any relation to the Montand side of the family," Cillay said. "But I suppose she might be a relative of my uncle's."

"Don't act like a servant, exactly," Adam Gary said. "Leastwise, not like servants used to act. Guess they're a dying breed."

"That's one I wish was. Dying breed, I mean. She was in my room this afternoon when I went upstairs to get a handkerchief," Mrs. Sanding said, with some indignation. "I asked her what she was doing and she said just checking to see that everything had been cleaned properly. Now, I ask you, she did it herself three days ago, so why would she need to check back today?"

"Nosy," Miss Appleton agreed, her blue head nodding. "Oh, she's got a shifty eye, that one has. I don't leave any valuables lying around in the open. I wouldn't put it past her to . . ."

Beatrice had come along the hall, and the conversation faltered. She gave no indication of realizing that she had been the object of discussion, merely nodding at Cillay.

"Would you mind calling your sister down to set the table? That task would be within her grasp, I take it?"

It wasn't the request, but the way she made it, the tone of voice, that bothered Cillay. As if Pam were somehow beneath contempt. She felt her own color rise, but moved immediately to the stairs, her voice kept level. "Yes, certainly. I'll call her."

On the second floor landing she collided, because she was angry and a bit upset at Beatrice's attitude and was not watching where she was going, with Mr. Chellmand. His hands shot out toward her shoulders, for the impact nearly threw her backward on the stairs.

"Watch it, you'll break your neck." He had a nice voice, deep, quiet, although at the moment it held a bit of annoyance. "Or someone else's. So you didn't take my advice, to look for a room somewhere else."

Cillay drew slightly away from him so that he had to drop his hands. "I couldn't, very well," she told him. "I'd . . . we, my sister and I . . . we've come to live with my aunt, Mrs. Pomeroy."

"Your aunt?" Had someone else reacted some-

34

what oddly when met with this information? She couldn't remember who, and the reaction was really rather slight, only a momentary stiffening of the face, a brief expression in the eyes that might not have been an expression at all, only a trick of the light.

"Why did you suggest that I go somewhere else?"

The tanned, handsome face was bland now. "Only that this is a house of old people, no place for a young girl. You'll die of boredom."

"But there's Mr. Creighton, isn't there? He isn't old."

The wide, thin lipped mouth twitched. "Oh, you've already met Alan? No, you're right. He is very, very young indeed. Excuse me, please," and he moved around her and went on down the stairs, leaving her in a pleasantly confused state. She had been very close to him for a moment, and the scent of his shaving lotion lingered; the pressure of his hands was still felt on her shoulders.

Had that actually been the reason he'd told her to leave this house, because it was full of old people? It seemed an odd thing to say to a perfect stranger, with no more reason than that.

She went on up after Pam, who had only recently awakened from her nap and was brushing her hair in front of the mirror. Cillay paused, her heart constricting as it sometimes did on seeing her sister at some simple task such as this. She was a remarkably pretty child, her slender body ripening into womanly curves with a promise that would never be fulfilled. Poor Pam . . . what lay ahead of her through the years? Never a lover, a husband, a child . . . all the things Cillay wanted most for herself. Would it lessen her own chances at happiness, being responsible for Pam? She was determined to keep the promise her mother had extracted from her, never to allow Pam to be placed in an institution. She was strong and healthy and thought she ought to be able to take care of her sister, but she couldn't help, sometimes, worrying about what would happen to the younger girl if she herself were to become ill or to die first.

Pam turned, seeing her in the mirror, her face lighting in the slow smile that was always so trusting, so sweet.

"Aunt Elsa would like you to set the table, Pam. Would you like to do that? Miss Appleton has picked some flowers to put in the center, I think, and it will be very pretty."

Pam liked pretty things . . . fabrics, flowers, costume jewelry. She came willingly enough, and when it was explained that she was to set a place for each of the chairs around the great oval table Cillay thought it was safe to leave her alone to do it.

Perhaps Alan Creighton would be coming home soon . . . surely he would if he were to eat dinner with the rest of them. Perhaps Mr. Chellmand would be there also, this time.

The roomers were all gathered in the front parlor (apparently the back one with its color television was Aunt Elsa's exclusive domain) when Cillay entered. Even Mr. Chellmand was there, reading the evening paper. He glanced up at her, briefly, with no more than a nod; so much for little girls.

Mrs. Sanding was playing solitaire on a card table set up in the front bay window, where she could watch the sidewalk as well as what went on in here.

She bobbed her head, smiling in greeting, and Mrs. Fontana lifted a mass of pink wool off one end of the sofa so that Cillay might sit down there if she wished.

But she wasn't interested in these people . . . Well, she was interested in Mr. Chellmand, but when he made such a point of treating her as a child . . . Anyway, she shook her head at Mrs. Fontana and went back out to the front door.

It was too chilly to sit on the steps for long, she discovered, for the sun had dropped behind the buildings now, but perhaps he would come soon . . .

He did, loping along the street with an armful of books, tripping over a shoe lace and stopping to tie it before he saw her. His face lit up in a gratifying way as he came through the gate, pushing it carelessly closed behind him.

"Hi! You know, I didn't find out your name this afternoon!"

She told him and he dropped onto the steps beside her. "Hey, that's really pretty . . . Cillay. Are you going to be here long?"

"I'm going to live here, I think. I hadn't anywhere else to go, you see, when my mother died. There was only Aunt Elsa . . . She's my father's sister. We'd never met her . . . She had a falling out with Daddy years ago over something nobody remembers any more . . . but when Mama asked if we could come to her, Pam and I, she agreed right away. Why are you living here? Don't you have a family, either?"

He ran a hand through his thick, fair hair. "Oh, gosh, yes, parents and two brothers and three sisters! But I'm going to school here, see, at City U. and there aren't enough dormitories, so over half the kids live off campus. It's hard to find a decent place at a reasonable price."

"Is this? I mean, decent and a reasonable price?"

"Oh, the price is high, but I guess they all are, from what the kids say. And it's old fashioned, but a buddy of mine lives in a place that has rats, and this one doesn't . . . It's OK, or it would be if the food were better. I only eat dinner here, so it's not as bad as if this was all I ever got." He flushed then, recalling that he was criticizing her aunt.

She smiled to let him know she didn't resent his remark. "It's so different here, from where we lived before. Serling is a small town, and we weren't so . . . alone. I don't know anyone here at all."

"You know me now," Alan said. He reached over to twist her wrist so that he could tell the time. "And if you know your aunt, you know it annoys her to have people come to the table late. I better run and put on a shirt . . . I don't think she approves of sweatshirts at dinner, either. See you later, Cillay."

She rose to follow him into the house. He was a nice boy, much like those she had known in high school. She already felt less alien in this house, knowing he was here.

Pam had done a lovely job on the table, and the china and the silver were nice things. There was a roast of lamb, poorly seasoned, and everything that went with it was just a little less tasty than it ought to have been. Beatrice was one of those people who have no instinct whatever about cooking.

The homemade bread, however, made a big hit; everyone ate several thick slices of it and Cillay, surreptitiously keeping track, saw that Mr. Chellmand and Alan each managed to down four slices. She brought in the cookies for dessert, and everyone except Mr. Chellmand complimented her on them.

Cillay had hoped to find time during the evening to get better acquainted with Alan, but Beatrice developed a headache and so Cillay was left to clean up the kitchen alone. She did so, with Pam contributing in a minor way by wiping silverware.

As she was about to go upstairs—it was late enough so that she thought she ought to get Pam started in the bath—she noticed that her aunt had put down her box of chocolates on a chair near the door. Elsa Pomeroy seldom went anywhere without her box of chocolates, and Cillay suspected she would want to nibble on a few before she went to bed. She sent her sister on upstairs with instructions to start taking a bath, and she herself went along the corridor to Mrs. Pomeroy's room.

The door was closed, and as she raised her hand to knock she heard their voices. Beatrice spoke with more emotion than she had so far expressed in Cillay's hearing: she was angry, and forceful, and because of this, perhaps, spoke more loudly than usual. At any rate, her voice came clearly through the wooden paneling.

"We've got to do something about her, Pet! Maybe you're willing to take a chance, but I'm not! You can't be so stupid you don't see how dangerous it can be!"

She couldn't understand her aunt's reply, but Beatrice's return was again loud enough to carry through the door.

"This is no time for that, you fool, can't you see we

risk everything if she stumbles onto anything! How can we be sure she won't?"

Cillay's hand was suspended in air, a few inches from the door. Who were they talking about? What was dangerous? Could the *she* Beatrice referred to, by any chance, be *herself?* For she was the only newcomer in the house, she and Pam.

Gradually, of its own volition, her hand was lowered and she began to back away from the door. If she knocked now they might suspect that she had overheard part of their conversation, and Beatrice's voice frightened her. When she said *we've got to do something about her,* it had a sinister sound, as if the *something* might be most unpleasant.

Her heart hammering, she retreated to the kitchen, put the chocolate box down where it had been, and crept silently up the stairs.

Chapter 4

Breakfast was the usual dreary affair, with neither
Mr. Chellmand nor Alan present to liven it up. Miss
Appleton was obviously setting herself to attract Mr.
Gary, and she blushed and laughed a lot, as if she
were a young girl with her first beau. Cillay might
have been amused, but she had not slept well and she
was tired; on top of that, she couldn't put out of her
mind the things she had heard Beatrice say last night.
She wished, belatedly, that she had, instead of running away, put an ear to the door so that she'd been
able to pick up her aunt's responses, as well.

There was a bit of excitement when, in the middle
of the morning, Mrs. Sanding called her to the back
door.

"Cillay, can you come and help? Beatrice has
taken a fall, I suspect she's broken her ankle! She
was going down the steps with a load of papers for
the incinerator, and must not have been able to see
where she was stepping! She's knocked her head, too,
poor thing!"

Beatrice had indeed taken a tumble; the contents
of the wastebaskets she had been carrying were scat-
tered over the little back yard, and the woman herself, half-sat, half-lay on the ground, her face twisted
with pain.

The ankle was already grossly swollen; there was
no question of her walking on it. Cillay and Mrs.

Sanding attempted to move her themselves and found it to be impossible. She was larger than either of them and their efforts brought a white line around Beatrice's mouth and a muttered oath.

"No, you can't do it! Get someone else to help . . . I think Mr. Chellmand came in a few minutes ago . . . !"

Cillay ran up the back stairs, reaching the second floor before she realized that she didn't know which room was his. She paused in the middle of the corridor, heart pounding from the exercise, and called out uncertainly, "Mr. Chellmand? Are you here?"

A door opened, only a few feet away, and he appeared. He was dressed as if he were going out, and he had a briefcase in his hand.

"Yes? Is something wrong?"

"Beatrice has had a fall, and we think she's broken her ankle. She's too heavy for us to lift . . ."

"All right. I'll be down in a minute, let me put this thing aside . . ." He disappeared briefly, reappearing without the case; Cillay noted that he checked to make sure his door had locked behind him. Which was, no doubt, only sensible in a rooming house, where you couldn't possibly know about the trustworthiness of your fellow roomers. "Let's go. Where is she?"

By the time they reached the back yard Mrs. Pomeroy was there, having waddled down the steps with considerable difficulty, for she was too fat to move either easily or quickly.

"Is it broken? It looks terrible," she observed, raising her eyes to Mr. Chellmand's.

He knelt to examine it at closer range. "It could be merely a bad sprain; they often swell quickly that way. Or that could be bone sticking out there . . . the only way to find out is to get her to a hospital and have it x-rayed. She certainly can't walk on it."

"A hospital! Oh, my lord! What do you think, Beatrice? Shall we take you to a hospital?"

Beatrice grimaced in pain and ill temper. "Well, I can't lie here forever, I hope. Do something!"

"I'm on my way to an important appointment, or I'd take you myself," Mr. Chellmand said. "But if the young lady would call a taxi I'll carry her out front and you can go to the hospital that way."

Cillay was dispatched to telephone, and by the time Beatrice had been carried carefully around the house the cab was waiting; the driver and Mr. Chellmand together maneuvered her into it.

"Someone will have to go with her," Chellmand observed. "It had better be you, hadn't it, Mrs. Pomeroy? Can you go the way you are?"

For a moment she resisted; the extent of her exertion was plain, for she wiped the perspiration from her fleshy face and her breath was coming in gasps. Sitting in front of a television set, eating chocolates, was poor preparation for any sort of physical activity.

"But I can't leave the house . . . It's almost time to begin lunch . . ."

"The girl can fix lunch better than you can," Beatrice snapped. "Come on, get in, he's right. They'll expect someone to fill out their damned forms and this hurts like fury . . . Come *on*, Pet!"

43

"Mr. Chellmand can't possibly go . . . ?" Mrs. Pomeroy still hesitated, and her lodger shook his head.

"I'm sorry . . . this is an important appointment, and I've got to run. You're all settled now; all you need is to get her there. It won't take long . . . and I'm sure the young lady can manage nicely for lunch. Can't you?"

Only Cillay could see his face when he turned to her, and there was something in it . . . it seemed that he compelled her to agree, that there was a warning, or was it a plea, in his green eyes.

"Yes, of course," Cillay responded, for anyone could match Beatrice's previous culinary efforts; and so Mrs. Pomeroy was bundled into the cab . . . almost as difficult a process as getting Beatrice in with her wounded foot . . . and the taxi roared off down the street.

"Well, I'll get my case and be off," the tall man said, and went back into the house; by the time Cillay and Mrs. Sanding and Mr. Gary, who had come out on hearing the commotion, had reached the house he was already back with his case, waving a careless hand in recognition of their presence.

Mrs. Sanding was smiling, whether in pleasure at the unexpected diversion or anticipation of a lunch not prepared by Beatrice was uncertain. "Do you want me to help you, my dear? It's been years since I pottered about a kitchen, but I still like to eat, so let's make the most of this, shall we?"

They looked over the supplies quickly, and Cillay decided on potato soup as being possible to produce in a limited amount of time and with the ingredients on hand. Miss Appleton came along, too, not to lend a hand, necessarily, but to have events explained to her. She then stood at the back window looking out at the disaster area.

"Someone ought to pick up all those papers she dumped and see that they're put into the incinerator, or they'll be all over the neighborhood, and then we'll have trouble for sure," she commented.

Cillay had forgotten about that mess. And as she was the only one in the house, except Pam, capable of bending and stooping, it had better be her task. She settled Mrs. Sanding at the sink with a batch of potatoes to peel, and called her sister to help her pick up the papers.

They had, indeed, blown all about, but because of the high fences she didn't think much, if anything, had escaped into the neighboring yards. She began to scoop them up and cram them into one of the wastebaskets lying on the walk.

She had no particular interest in what had come out of anyone's wastebasket, and paid little attention to what she handled; the papers seemed mostly old bills and letters and tissues. She was almost finished when she put her hand on a full sized sheet of paper and was about to thrust it into the basket after the others when she stopped.

The entire page was covered with a name, written over and over, as if someone were practicing penmanship. She recognized the rather shaky writing; it was the same as on the letter her mother had gotten from Aunt Elsa. And the name repeated so many times was Elsa S. Pomeroy.

Why on earth would Aunt Elsa be practicing writing her own name? On the heels of that thought came another. Was someone *else* trying to copy her signature? She stood looking at the writing for another moment or two, then poked it into the basket with the others. Probably Aunt Elsa had simply doodled her name, the way some people do with little sketches, perhaps while she was telephoning or listening to someone talk.

She didn't forget it, however, and she wondered if Beatrice might not be above a spot of forgery, if she thought she could get away with it. Maybe Cillay ought to mention it to her aunt when she came home, just in case.

She had gone back into the house and was going in search of Pam to help in the dining room when a rather curious thing happened. Mrs. Pomeroy's room, and the one that belonged to Beatrice, were off one of the short passageways at the back of the house. With both of these people away, there should have been no one in that area at all. Yet as she moved along the main corridor she heard the distinct sound of something . . . a door? a drawer? being closed.

Cillay's reaction was instinctive; she never considered the possibility that it might be dangerous to investigate the unexpected sound. She walked down the hall toward her aunt's room. The carpeting was thin, here, and did not completely muffle her footsteps; she had made no effort to be quiet.

The sound was repeated . . . behind the closed door she heard the furtive closing of what was probably a dresser drawer. She reached for the knob, intending to throw open the door and confront the in-

46

truder. No one had any business in there, she thought indignantly, while Aunt Elsa was out . . .

As her hand closed around the brass knob she heard the unmistakable click of the lock.

Cillay stared at the door, astonished. Someone had heard her coming and deliberately stopped her from entering!

In the silence there were no sounds from the street, no sounds in the house itself . . . only, when she held her own breath, she knew that someone else waited with suspended breath on the other side of the door.

If anything were stolen, it would be her fault . . . She was in charge of the house now. She stood irresolute, wondering what to do. She could call Mr. Chellmand, as the only able-bodied male in the place . . . but no, he had hurried off to his appointment. And Alan was in school . . . would frail old Mr. Gary be of any use?

For lack of any better solution, she decided to tell Mrs. Sanding; perhaps she'd know what they ought to do.

Again her heels were audible on the floor, but she didn't care. She fairly flew back to the kitchen, where the two old ladies were amiably dicing up the potatoes as she had instructed.

"Is this enough, do you think?"

She scarcely looked at the pot Mrs. Sanding held out for her inspection, because through the kitchen window she caught a glimpse of a dark head moving in the direction of the rear of the lot.

Mr. Chellmand. Mr. Chellmand, who was sup-

47

posedly at an important engagement somewhere else. To make absolutely sure, Cillay moved to the door to look after him, but she caught only a glimpse of a man in dark clothes disappearing around the corner of the garage.

Had it been Mr. Chellmand?

She could never swear to it. She hadn't seen his face, only the upper part of a dark head of hair.

"Is something wrong, dear?" Mrs. Sanding was asking, and she drew a deep breath and tried to compose herself.

"No, I only have to check on something . . . would you cut up the celery, too, and I'll be right back."

This time the knob turned easily under her hand. The room, as she had expected, was empty, but she confirmed her impression that there was a window opening on that side of the house, and it was without a screen. She pushed at it, and it rose without a sound and lowered again the same way.

There was no way of knowing whether or not anything had been taken. She glanced around the room, but the clutter was so great . . . the desk was a jumble of papers and the inevitable box of chocolates. It looked pretty much the same as it had when she'd been in here before.

There was nothing she could do. She knew she ought to report the incident when her aunt returned, but she shrank from doing so. She couldn't implicate a roomer without any more evidence than she had, at any rate.

Thoughtfully, Cillay made her way back to the

kitchen, her uneasiness growing. There was something not right about this house, but she didn't know what it was. She only knew that it was beginning to be frightening.

Chapter 5

Lunch was served on time, and everyone was there, including Beatrice and Mrs. Pomeroy. Beatrice did not have a fracture, only a severe sprain; her ankle was tightly wrapped in an elastic bandage, and she was to elevate the foot and on no condition to walk on it for several days.

Mr. Chellmand showed up, a few minutes late, sliding into his chair with a murmured apology. At first Cillay could not look at him, fearing that her suspicions would be written across her face for him to read; when she did raise her head he looked the same as before, reserved but perfectly ordinary. Not like a sneak thief, a prowler.

Cillay served her potato soup with a few sprigs of parsley and a pat of butter floating on each bowl, and it was so well received that everyone but Mrs. Fontana had a second helping. Mr. Gary patted Cillay on the arm and complimented her on it, saying that he hoped she'd take over all the cooking, which did seem, at the moment, quite likely.

She continued to observe Mr. Chellmand surreptitiously as he drained his soup bowl. His clothes were well cut, of good quality, and the cuff links he wore looked expensive. What, she wondered, was he doing in a place like this? He looked more the sort of man to have an apartment of his own, with a built-in bar and etchings to show to attractive blondes.

Once he looked up and caught her eyes on him; she flushed faintly but his face remained enigmatic.

"I suppose you know, my dear," Mrs. Pomeroy addressed her, "that we're going to have to depend on you to keep us fed until poor Beatrice can get around again. I'm afraid I can't move about too much, either. My heart, you know," and she patted her enormous bosom.

Cillay nodded numbly. Mrs. Sanding chuckled. "Ah, well, if she can make bread and soup like this, we won't starve, will we?"

If Beatrice realized that her own cooking was being criticized, she gave no indication of it. She had been provided with a crutch, which she handled awkwardly. When she had eaten she maneuvered herself out of the dining room and went to her bedroom to take another of her pain pills and lie down, she said.

When Cillay took stock of the kitchen supplies, she was appalled at how little there was to work with. When she approached her aunt in the television room, where the woman was already sucking chocolates half an hour after lunch, she requested permission to obtain more supplies.

"Beatrice usually does the shopping, but it's certain she can't, now. We shop at the market on Thirty-Third Street, four blocks over," Mrs. Pomeroy told her. "If you'll fetch my purse I'll give you some money and you can walk over . . . perhaps your sister could help carry things."

It was fun to be out, walking briskly along the walk, listening to Pam's childish chatter about the houses and the gardens they passed, not letting herself think about the peculiarities of her aunt's household. Fortunately, she liked to cook, and even if she hadn't, a chance to get away from Beatrice's unimaginative fare would have been some incentive. She found the market without difficulty and began, carefully and thriftily, to select her purchases.

The proprietor, who also served as the butcher, added up her order of roasts, chops, soup meat, and ground beef, looking at her curiously.

"Haven't seen you in the neighborhood before, have I?"

"No. I've come to live with my aunt, Mrs. Pomeroy, on Hillsdale Street."

"Mrs. Pomeroy? That the lady that used to have the boarding house?"

Used to have? "She still has it," Cillay told him, counting out the money.

"Oh, she got better, eh? That's good. Glad to hear it."

Cillay stood with her palm out for the change, somewhat confused. "I don't . . . was she sick? I didn't know."

"Oh, I heard Mrs. Pomeroy was sick and had to close down the place, must be two months ago. I knew one of her boarders, fellow by the name of Acheson, he was pretty upset about having to find another place to live. He'd lived there fifteen years, almost. But they all had to go, and not much notice about it, either, from what I understood. Gave 'em all a week to find other places. Not easy, you know, to find a place in a week."

Cillay lifted the sack down from the top of the counter and handed it to Pam, completely puzzled.

When Aunt Elsa had written to her mother three months ago there had been no suggestion that she was ill. Of course anything could have happened since then, but the rooming house was nearly full now.

It occurred to her, on the way home, that the unknown Mr. Acheson might in some way have become undesirable, so that her aunt had made an excuse of closing down the house rather than asking him outright to leave. Yes, that must be it, she decided, and let herself be drawn back to Pam's level of conversation.

They walked slowly through the golden September afternoon, enjoying the warmth of it. A boy, strolling home from school, glanced admiringly at them, but Cillay saw that his eyes lingered longest on Pam.

Pam, the innocent . . . how much of a job would it be, protecting her from men who might find her attractive in spite of her mental retardation? Pam would never know what one wanted of her, should his motives be dishonorable, and she was so pliable and complacent that she would probably go along with whatever anyone suggested to her. In a way, she supposed that an institution might be safer . . . But she had promised her mother that Pam would never be put away, never locked up in one of those places. Not so long as Cillay was able to do anything about caring for her.

The sacks were heavy and Pam was complaining by the time they reached home. They put away their purchases, and upon discovering a spice cupboard Cillay found that it was already well stocked with

53

seasonings. Someone, at some time, had evidently known how to use spices and herbs. She wondered who it had been.

Mrs. Sanding poked her head around the corner. "Want any help? No? Well, I'm not really all that energetic, I only hoped you were planning something better than that dreadful lamb roast for dinner." She waited hopefully, her eyes bright, her head cocked to one side.

"I thought tonight we'd have pork chops. I know a way to bake them in a cream sauce with herbs. And perhaps baked potatoes . . ."

"Ah, very good! You know, I'd never have come here if I'd known how dreadful the food would be. I've thought of moving again, but good boarding houses aren't all that easy to find, and it's so difficult to move . . . I have to do it by taxi, you see, and I remember how horrid it was, only six weeks ago."

"Oh, have you only been here for six weeks? I thought you all seemed like such old friends . . . so comfortable with one another." Cillay stretched to place a box on a high shelf.

"Oh, gracious, none of us has been here long, you know. Mr. Gary came just before I did, and Mrs. Fontana and Miss Appleton within a week or so of me. Mr. Chellmand's only been here about two weeks, and that boy . . . Alan . . . came right when school started. Of course it doesn't take long to get acquainted when you've nothing to do but sit around all day and compare life histories."

Cillay felt her arm paralyzed, held over her head. Six weeks, or a little more? Surely that was curious,

54

when her aunt had been operating a boarding house for so long, that all the tenants would move out at once, and a whole new batch move in a few weeks later? Of course the butcher had said the place had been closed because Mrs. Pomeroy was ill . . .

She finished putting away the groceries, scarcely listening to Mrs. Sanding's prattle. It was quite likely that it had happened just that way, that her aunt had taken ill and thought it to be more serious than it was; when she'd recovered she had naturally advertised for new roomers. That was all.

She caught Mr. Chellmand's name somewhere in the monologue going on. "What's his other name? Mr. Chellmand's? And what does he do?"

The old lady wrinkled her forehead. "Sam. His name's Sam. I think he's an insurance man or something like that. He never gets any mail. Not a single piece since he's been here, isn't that strange? Not that the rest of us get much, but we're old, don't have any families left. It's sad to be old and no family left, I tell you."

It's sad to be young and no family left, Cillay thought, but didn't say it. And then, some time later, she realized that she did have some family; she had Aunt Elsa.

"I can't imagine why that boy came here," Mrs. Sanding went on, apparently untroubled by Cillay's lack of response. "This isn't the sort of place you'd think a young man would come. So dull, you know, and the food so tasteless. Although now that woman is crippled, at least we'll eat decently for a time."

Cillay found that cooking for ten people was more time consuming than cooking for three had been, but

55

there were more compensations, too. These people were all so delighted with whatever she fixed that she put herself out to please them. She was afraid, when her aunt saw the desserts she had prepared with real whipped cream topping, that there might be a complaint about the cost; but Elsa Pomeroy had a well developed sweet-tooth and even suggested to Cillay that in the future a second dessert might be held back for her, so that she might have it as an evening snack. She did inquire about the cost, but seemed satisfied when Cillay told her.

Alan Creighton managed to corner Cillay that evening before she went up to bed. She was tired, and had already sent Pam upstairs, but she paused to talk to him. The hallway was the only reasonably private place, as Mrs. Pomeroy was ensconced on the sofa in the TV room and the others were playing solitaire (Mrs. Sanding), knitting (Mrs. Fontana), or giggling together over something in the evening paper (Mr. Gary and Miss Appleton).

Cillay and Alan sat on the lower stairs, talking about themselves for a time; she explained that she had had one year of college but didn't expect to be able to get any more, although she hoped eventually to be able to get a job and take care of her sister. Alan was studying to be a P.E. teacher, he told her, and maybe make the first string on the football team by next year.

And then, suddenly, he took a different tack. "What do you know about your aunt, Cillay?"

"Know about her?" She was seated on a higher step than he; she gazed down at him curiously. "I don't know what you mean. She's my father's sister. That's all."

"I mean . . . well, you don't really know much about what sort of person she is, I guess."

"No. Except that she was kind enough to offer to take us in. I'm very grateful for that. If there had been only me to consider I could have gotten a job back in Serling, I think, and made enough to support myself. But I don't know enough about anything to get a good paying position right off, and I suspect I couldn't support two of us, especially if I have to pay a sitter. I can't leave Pammy alone. So it's marvelous that we have a place to stay for a while."

"Yeah. I guess so." He sounded subdued, and soon changed the subject, and Cillay was glad enough to go to bed soon afterward, for she had to be up early to prepare breakfast.

Perhaps it was because she had worked hard that day, and was especially tired. Sometimes when one is overtired sleep refuses to come. At any rate, Cillay tossed and turned restlessly for some time on the narrow bed.

Alan's studiedly casual question about her aunt took on sinister overtones. The sheet on which someone had practiced Aunt Elsa's signature loomed somehow more significant than before. But most of all, she kept reliving that moment outside Mrs. Pomeroy's door, when she heard the lock click and sensed another presence there, listening, as she was listening.

Had she imagined that the intruder had gone out through a window? If it were someone who belonged in the house, he might easily have unlocked the door as soon as she was gone. Only, of course, he would have no way of knowing whether she had retreated any further than the main hall, where she could watch for him to leave.

So, the window. How many of the lodgers here were agile enough to climb out a window? Certainly none of the old ladies could have done it. She wasn't so sure about Mr. Gary. He was elderly but quite spry. She couldn't picture Mr. Gary snooping about in someone else's belongings, however.

Alan had been at school. While Sam Chellmand, who had been instrumental in seeing that Mrs. Pomeroy went along to the hospital with Beatrice, had been absent on his own business.

Or had he? Might he not have circled back, while they were all busy in the kitchen, and entered Aunt Elsa's room? How could she know if the dark head she had seen passing the window had indeed been Sam Chellmand? The only thing she could say for sure was that it could *not* have been either Alan or Mr. Gary.

Eventually she fell into a deep sleep, and, as is sometimes the way at such times, her dreams were particularly vivid.

She dreamed that men had come for Pam, to take her away to a place with gray walls and bars on the windows; men who jerked at her arms and paid no attention to her piteous cries. And Mama was watching, with tears streaming down her face, pleading with Cillay not to let them do it.

And then Pam was gone, and Cillay was alone in this great house with only Aunt Elsa, only she was a changed, evil form now. The house interior was composed of spider webs, thick, dusty, too tough to break through. And there in the center of the webs was Aunt Elsa; a fat, shining black widow spider, who never moved but watched everything while she sucked the insides out of gigantic black chocolates.

Cillay woke, gasping, sweating, shivering. It was some time before her pulses subsided enough to enable her to go back to sleep. And when she woke the next morning she remembered the dreams, and was uneasy.

Chapter 6

She was used to the back stairs by now; narrow and ill-lit as they were, she took them at a fairly rapid pace, for there were no obstructions.

That is, there never had been any obstructions, until this morning.

The bottom of the enclosed staircase was usually illuminated by the light from the kitchen, for the door would be left standing open. This morning someone had carelessly closed it, so that the lower dozen steps were in almost total darkness, but Cillay hurried anyway, for after her fitful night she had been slow in dressing.

Something caught her legs, something hard and unyielding, and she pitched forward down the remainder of the stairs, striking her head on the door hard enough so that her vision blurred momentarily. The door was immediately pulled open from the other side, and Sam Chellmand stood there looking down at her. She recognized his large, well polished shoes, for she was temporarily unable to lift her head to see any more.

"Are you hurt?" His voice was not as curt as usual; he knelt beside her and helped her to a sitting position on the kitchen floor. "Don't try to move unless you're sure. You'll have to learn to come down stairs more carefully."

"There was something . . ." It hurt to talk, for

she had bitten her tongue; she tasted the blood. ". . . someone put something on the stairs."

He abandoned her long enough to verify this, coming back with the cause of her fall.

"A broom. What the hell was the broom doing on the stairs; isn't there a broom closet? It must have fallen sideways and become wedged in solid. You're going to have some good bruises, but have you broken anything?"

Her left shoulder ached, but she was able to use the arm. Still sitting on the floor, she examined her shins and could already discern the purplish marks where they had struck the broom handle.

"I think I'm all right," she decided. "Is my forehead turning purple, too?"

He had knelt beside her again; gently, his fingers touched her chin, tilting her head so that he could examine it. "I'm afraid so. Are you sure you want to try to stand up?"

She did so, with his help, relieved to find that everything functioned albeit somewhat painfully. "Thank you. Lucky for me you were here . . ."

Her voice trailed off, as it occurred to her to wonder what he was doing in the kitchen at seven o'clock in the morning. He would not normally have been there at any hour. His eyes met hers, and he knew what she was thinking; his mouth quirked and his eyebrows rose, conveying a message without speaking a word: *you aren't going to tell anyone, are you?*

They heard her coming, for Mrs. Pomeroy rustled when she moved, and weakened floorboards creaked under her weight. She eased her bulk through the doorway and surveyed them.

"I heard an awful racket . . . what is it?"

"Cillay fell downstairs. Some idiot had stuck a broom there instead of in the broom closet, and she tripped over it. She's banged up, but nothing seriously damaged, apparently," Sam Chellmand said easily. "I heard her and came to investigate."

Suggesting that he had come from the front of the house, from an area where he had a right to be, which was an outright misrepresentation, Cillay thought numbly, massaging her shoulder. He had been right on the other side of that door.

"You can get breakfast all right?" Mrs. Pomeroy demanded, rather anxiously. It was clear that she had no desire to take over that task, herself.

"Oh, yes, I'm sure I can. I'd better get started, or everyone will be late."

"Alan eats at the school cafeteria, I understand, and he's already gone," Sam Chellmand informed her. "And I'll be eating out, too, so that only leaves the old ladies and Mr. Gary, who aren't in any hurry to go anywhere. Slow down, before you manage to kill yourself."

Satisfied that she was not needed, Mrs. Pomeroy waddled back to her bedroom to dress, for she was presently encased in a stunning rose satin dressing gown. Sam Chellmand hesitated a moment, looking down at Cillay.

"I mean it, young lady. Be careful in this house."

She wanted to ask him if he had been the one behind that locked door yesterday, but she could not bring herself to form the words. She wanted to know, too, why he was in the kitchen, but he gave her no

62

explanation, only a small, encouraging smile, before he left her there.

If she hadn't so thoroughly cleaned and organized the kitchen herself she might not have noticed the small changes this morning, but it was soon fairly obvious that Sam Chellmand had been there by design. He had been searching for something.

Drawers had been pulled out and slightly disarranged. Various articles had been shifted in the cupboards, as if they'd been moved so that he could see behind them. Dish towels had been lifted and put back less tidily.

Had he rifled Aunt Elsa's room yesterday and tried again here this morning? But that wasn't likely, was it? Who keeps valuables hidden in the flour bin or behind jars of preserves? On second thought, an old woman might do that, she supposed, but this kitchen seemed an unlikely spot to look for money, or jewels, or anything of that nature. And if anything had been missing from her room wouldn't Aunt Elsa have noticed it and said something by this time?

Besides, there was something about Sam Chellmand . . . she could not believe he was a sneak thief. Or was it, she thought guiltily, that she didn't want to believe such a thing?

Breakfast was only a few minutes later than usual, and as it was of much improved flavor and quality no one seemed to mind. Cillay watched her aunt forking omelet greedily into her mouth, remembering her dream of the spider consuming chocolates, and fought down her repugnance. So the old woman was rather unattractive, padded in all that fat; she had, the fact remained, been generous enough to open her home to two nieces she'd never seen in her life.

"I was wondering," Mrs. Fontana said, patting her lips delicately with her paper napkin, "if our rooms are going to vacuumed and dusted this week? With Miss Beatrice injured, I mean? The weather's been so warm I've had the windows open rather a lot, and my room is *quite* dusty, I'm afraid."

"Wouldn't break her arm to dust it herself," Mrs. Sanding muttered, *sotto voce,* and was as usual ignored.

Mrs. Pomeroy contemplated another sausage and decided that she could hold it; while she masticated she shifted her attention to Cillay.

"Do you think you could manage that? There isn't all that much to do, everyone's responsible for his own room except for vacuuming once a week, and light dusting."

Cillay thought with some concern of the dishes and the preparations to be made so soon for lunch, but perhaps she could trust Pam with the dishes, especially as she hadn't used the best china for breakfast.

"I'll certainly try," she agreed, deciding privately to do Mrs. Fontana's room first in the belief that the others wouldn't be nearly so critical if it weren't done promptly and thoroughly.

Pam, intrigued by the mountains of frothy suds, was settled at the kitchen sink. Heaven only knew how much actual washing she would do, but surely most of the dishes would soak clean while she played in the water. Cillay dragged out the bulky vacuum cleaner and hauled it up the front stairs.

Miss Fontana's room was a neater replica of Aunt Elsa's. There was the same old fashioned furniture, and the accumulation of years of china figurines and bric-a-brac. She had installed bookcases but they were innocent of books, holding instead all these little shepherds and shepherdesses, china elves and fairies, fawns and stags and horses and lambs. Cillay stared at them in dismay, for they were, indeed, covered with a visible film of dust. Surely she wasn't required to dust all of those?

Mrs. Sanding had come to the doorway behind her and followed her gaze. "I wouldn't worry about 'em," she said. "Let her dust her own dohickeys, I say. She knows Beatrice can't get up here, and you've got your hands full in the kitchen. I'd rather eat well than have somebody dusting all that junk, I'll tell you. Lord, hasn't she got a mess of it? Junk, I mean?"

"I'm afraid they'll have to wait until I've vacuumed all the rooms, at least," Cillay decided.

She plugged in the cleaner and began to use it. Its sound didn't deter Mrs. Sanding from continuing to talk, raising her voice above the noise.

"All that pink yarn . . . she must've gotten a terrific bargain on it, she's got thirty skeins! What do you suppose she's making all that stuff for, she hasn't even got any children or grandchildren left to make it for, and she's got two pink sweaters herself already." She had come on into the room and before Cillay could think what to do to stop her had picked up a small folder . . . a bank book? . . . from the top of the desk. "Good grief, look at this!"

"Mrs. Sanding, I don't think we ought to . . ."

Her voice failed when she looked down at the open book the old lady was holding in front of her.

"Sixty-two thousand and twelve dollars! Lord, if I had that kind of money I wouldn't be staying in a place like this! Although some of those fancy rest homes are little more than prisons, from what I hear, and the food no better than it was here before you took over . . . Sixty-two thousand dollars! My lord! No wonder she can afford to buy thirty skeins of pink wool!"

"We oughtn't to touch her things," Cillay said, swallowing. "I mean, they *are* private, you know."

Mrs. Sanding replaced the bank book on the desk. "Oh, well, what's so secret about having money in the bank? You know, I'm surprised she hasn't thrown it out as bait . . . she's interested in Adam Gary, too, you know! Oh, don't look at me that way. I've seen her watching him! But she doesn't play up to him the way that silly Elizabeth Appleton does. You'd think she'd give up, wouldn't you . . . Elizabeth, I mean . . . if she never got a man in eighty years wouldn't you think it was too late?"

Cillay pretended she couldn't hear because of the sound of the vacuum cleaner and hoped that neither of the ladies being discussed would hear the raised voice.

She had turned off the machine and was ready to dust . . . the flat surfaces of the room, not the collector's items . . . when she heard the front door bell peal.

"Oh, dear . . . I wonder, if it wouldn't be too much trouble, Mrs. Sanding, would you answer that?"

"Of course. And don't you worry about how good

a job of cleaning you can do today . . . we're all more interested in being fed than in a little bit of dust, I assure you." With that she scurried off down the stairs, and Cillay sighed in relief and hoped she would stay down stairs.

She knew immediately which was Miss Appleton's room, for it was just like its owner. All ruffles and frills and femininity. A great, elegantly dressed doll adorned the bed; there was a little love seat covered in pale blue velvet which was piled with souvenir pillows from Atlantic City and Pasadena and Miami Beach. Miss Appleton had been around, it seemed. She had no books, no papers, nothing to collect extra dust and make cleaning her room harder.

Mr. Gary's room was next, and he did have books, but they were in glass fronted cases so she didn't have to touch them. There were a few photographs, most of them very old, and half a dozen heavy photograph albums. His room was relatively uncluttered and there was nothing on the floor to obstruct the vacuum cleaner, so she finished there in a hurry.

She decided she had time for one more room before she began preparations for lunch, and as Sam Chellmand's room was next in order, she took that one. Except for the fact that he had an extra suit and a jacket and two pair of slacks in the closet, there was nothing in sight to indicate that the room was occupied. Of course Mrs. Sanding said he had not been here long, but it seemed that a man would have more belongings than these. She and Pam had each brought more than this with them on the bus.

She was most curious about Sam Chellmand, but she didn't know how to go about finding out anything. Anyone who could afford the sort of clothes he wore would be likely to be able to afford better living accommodations than a single old-fashioned room in a rooming house.

She finished the room, unplugged the vacuum, and had carried it into the hall when she paused. Because of her suspicions of him, was she justified in looking through his belongings to see if he had any identification, anything to prove that he was (or was not) a respectable citizen?

The temptation was strong, but her early training was stronger. Her mother would have been horrified that she could so much as contemplate such a thing. And besides, there probably was nothing to find, or he'd have locked his room today as he had done previously. Resolutely, Cillay hauled the cleaner to the end of the hallway, out of the line of traffic, and left it there.

Pam, after a period of several hours, had not completely washed the dishes, but she had had a lovely time in the suds, she said, and Cillay finished them up rapidly while Pam was put to work with a dish towel.

Mrs. Sanding came back to announce that the shipping company had delivered the rest of the girls' belongings and they were all stacked in the entryway, awaiting someone to carry them upstairs.

She stayed to chatter for a few minutes, mostly about Elizabeth Appleton, who had gone walking to display a new dress she had; she had induced (trapped, Mrs. Sanding implied) Mr. Gary to accompany her, and it was evident that Mrs. Sanding was inwardly seething.

"You ought to see the skirt on it! I ask you, how can a woman eighty years old wear a skirt that shows her knees? Miniskirts may be all right on teenagers, but on old women they're ridiculous!"

Actually, Miss Appleton's knees were not bad, Cillay thought, observing them when they all came in to lunch. But she wasn't about to antagonize Mrs. Sanding by saying so; she felt that Mrs. Sanding was, at the moment, the closest thing to a friend she had in this place.

It startled her to realize that she could not feel that way about Aunt Elsa. For all her seeming kindness, there was no genuine warmth in the woman. She was concerned with little beyond her own comfort and pleasure; the fact that she kept her roomers reasonably well satisfied was, Cillay thought, more for her own sake than theirs. If they were content, they would remain and pay their rent, which in turn contributed to the innumerable boxes of chocolates the woman consumed, and also to the television payments.

Beatrice hobbled in for lunch; judging by her face the pain was well controlled now so long as she put no weight on the injured foot. She several times requested some extra service from Cillay, and the girl began to wonder if Beatrice would have a lengthy recovery period. She had expected to help around the house, but she hadn't counted on being given all the work to do by herself.

By the time she had served dinner, she was exhausted. Pam helped in minor ways, but she was too simple minded to be given anything but the lowliest of tasks. Mr. Chellmand was not there for dinner, and Alan was eating out, too; if any of the others noticed that she was too tired to eat they didn't mention it.

She met Sam Chellmand in the hallway later in the evening, though; he spoke briefly and started to pass her, then paused and came back.

"What's the matter with you? You look ill."

"No. No, I'm not ill. It's only . . . I suppose I'm tired tonight."

His eyes narrowed, searching her face. "I guess you are. What the hell have they done, made you a work horse since Beatrice is out of commission? Isn't Mrs. Pomeroy doing anything at all?"

Cillay didn't reply, but the tell-tale flush of her cheeks was answer enough. His mouth flattened.

"Why did you come here? Haven't you anyone else you could go to?"

Silently, Cillay shook her head, embarrassed by his attention, yet grateful, too.

"No one at all? A godmother? A friend, somewhere?"

"Not really. I mean, only school friends . . . they couldn't . . . take us in, or anything like that." Her voice was husky, perhaps with fatigue.

"Money? Have you any money?"

"A little." She was ashamed to admit how little.

"How much?" He was waiting for her, he wasn't going to give up without getting a definite answer. Cillay lifted her head.

"About a hundred and twenty dollars."

He swore under his breath. "You don't belong in this house."

She was emboldened by his concern. "Why not, Mr. Chellmand? It's my aunt's house."

"It's an evil house. Can't you feel it? Can't you smell it?"

"I don't understand what you mean," she said, but in a way she was lying. She was uneasy here, she was worried about her future . . . hers and Pam's.

He stared at her, it seemed in exasperation, then touched her lightly on the shoulder. "Well. I suppose there's nothing I can do right now. But remember this . . . if anything happens to frighten you, tell me. You understand that? Come and tell me. I'm a little older than you are, with a good deal more experience . . . if you run into something you don't know how to handle, let me know."

This from the taciturn Sam Chellmand! She couldn't believe it.

"I don't expect it will be necessary, but . . . thank you, thank you very much," she told him sincerely. "That's very kind of you."

She didn't catch it, but as she mounted the stairs on her way to bed Sam Chellmand stared after her, noting the weary sag of her shoulders, the slim grace of her body, the graceful swing of her long brown hair.

"Kind, hell," he said under his breath, and watched her until she vanished around the corner.

Chapter 7

The days settled into a routine with little deviation. Cook, clean, cook, clean. Beatrice still sat around with her foot elevated, reading or watching television with Mrs. Pomeroy. Mrs. Pomeroy spoke only to ask for service or to criticize, mildly and lightly, when something was not done to her exact liking.

Pam was a problem. There wasn't enough for her to do. She would have enjoyed going to the park every afternoon to play on the swings (there was one only a few blocks away) but Cillay didn't have time to take her and could not trust her to go alone. She got coloring materials for her, but there was a limit to the number of hours the younger girl would spend at the kitchen table, sketching and coloring.

On top of this, Pam annoyed Beatrice. It was, Cillay thought, the irrational fear of one unused to mental retardation; Beatrice would jump when Pam appeared unexpectedly, and did not like to have the girl around her.

Once, when Pam had been cutting out paper dolls and went into the parlor to replace the scissors in the drawer where they belonged, Beatrice had half-risen in her chair, alarm clearly written on her face.

"Are you sure it's safe to let her have those things?" she demanded.

Cillay hastened to reassure her. "She's quite harmless, really she is! She isn't crazy, you know, it's only that she's like a little child! Please, don't be afraid of her."

"I'm not afraid of her," Beatrice said coldly, subsiding in her chair, but from then on Cillay took special pains to keep her sister away from the woman.

One afternoon Mrs. Pomeroy came to her with a request. She showed her a small bank passbook with a dark red cover . . . not the inside, but enough of a glimpse to know what it was.

"I seem to have mislaid my other bankbook. It has a blue cover, otherwise it's just like this one. Keep an eye out for it and bring it to me if you find it, will you? I can't imagine where I put it down, but it's around here somewhere."

Cillay agreed that she would watch for it. Several days later she did find it, tucked inside an old telephone book in a drawer in the kitchen. She noticed the date on the book, and wondered why it was being kept when it was obviously out of date; when she picked it up the little bank book fell out of it.

She had no sense of doing wrong when she opened it; her eyes noted the column listing the balance, and saw that at one time the account had held as much as fourteen thousand dollars. But it had been withdrawn over a period of several months, and the final withdrawal, which closed the account, had been made on the seventh of July . . . a little less than three months ago.

"What are you doing?"

Cillay spun about, feeling guilty although she really had no reason to do so. She held up the pass-

73

book in explanation. "Aunt Elsa asked me to keep an eye out for a bank book like this, and I just found one. But I don't think it's the one she wanted."

Beatrice crossed the kitchen rapidly in spite of her crutch and useless foot, and held out an imperious hand for the book. "Give it to me! It's none of your affair to look into other people's bank books! It is the one she's been hunting, and you're standing here poking into it instead of taking it to her!"

"But there's nothing in this account," Cillay pointed out, relinquishing the book. "See, it's been closed. So there must be another one."

She broke off at the expression of rage and disbelief on Beatrice's face. "It can't have been closed! There should be at least . . . She stopped, as if she had been trapped by her anger into saying too much. As she opened the book to verify the fact that the money had all been withdrawn from the account, her face was pale; Cillay thought there were drops of perspiration on her forehead, although those could have been from the exertion of hurrying when she could not walk properly.

"Maybe you're right. Maybe there is another one," Beatrice said, but her tone belied this. "Well, I'll take it to her anyway."

Cillay stood in the middle of the kitchen, her body trembling, and she could not control it immediately. She stooped to pick up the telephone book and its pages rattled in her hand until she put it on the counter.

Beatrice's venomous attack had been unfair. Cillay felt herself in a position of being unable to fight back against the older woman. Beatrice was established

74

here, her position stronger than that of an employee
. . . she always referred to Mrs. Pomeroy as "Pet"
and although she did as "Pet" ordered she at no time
acted as an inferior or in a subservient manner.

She smoothed out the crumpled pages of the telephone book, more to give her shaking fingers a chance
to relax than in hope of salvaging the book, for it
was over a year old. Witlessly, her eyes ran down
the page of names, and gradually an idea came to
her.

She turned the pages toward the front of the book,
then forced her finger to steady as it moved down the
column. *Chellmand, R. S.* Could that be it? Of course,
her Mr. Chellmand went by the name of Sam, but
the middle initial was *S.* and lots of people prefer to
use their middle names. She read it again. Chellmand, R. S. Attorney at law. There followed two
addresses, one presumably an office address, the other
a residence.

Looking quickly over her shoulder to make sure no
one was watching, Cillay tore out the corner of the
page containing the Chellmand name. It was the only
one in the book, and sufficiently unusual so that she
thought it must be either *her* man or a relative. Some-
time, when there was no one to listen in, she determined to call the two numbers and see what she
could find out.

Her opportunity came later in the day, when both
her aunt and Beatrice were napping. She was reasonably certain they were, for Beatrice had closed
herself into her room, and Mrs. Pomeroy could be
heard snoring.

She didn't want the roomers to hear her, either, but

they all appeared to be occupied with knitting or reading material, and she could hear Miss Appleton's girlish giggle occasionally.

The only telephone in the house was in the front hall. She thought she could talk from there without being overheard.

Carefully, she dialed the first number. There was a busy signal, so she dialed the residence number. A woman's voice replied, "Chellmand residence."

"Hello . . ." Why hadn't she planned what to say? "May . . . may I speak to Mr. Chellmand, please?"

"I'm sorry, Mr. Chellmand is out of town. May I ask who's calling, please?"

Cillay ignored the request. "Can you tell me when he'll be back?"

"I couldn't say for sure; perhaps a few weeks. May I have your name, please?"

A few weeks. If this Mr. Chellmand actually was out of town, he couldn't be *Sam*. Carefully, Cillay replaced the receiver, knowing she would get no more out of the woman without revealing herself, which she was not prepared to do.

Again she tried the first number, and this time another woman answered, in polished accents, "Mr. Chellmand's office. Who's calling, please?"

"I'm trying to get in touch with Mr. Chellmand," Cillay said, trying to sound older than she was. "Is he in, please?"

"No, I'm sorry, he isn't. May I take your name and have him call you?"

"But he is in town, then?"

"Oh, yes, certainly. I expect him later today. Did you want to make an appointment?"

"Well, I'm not sure I have the right party. Would this be Mr. *Sam* Chellmand?"

"Mr. Chellmand uses the name Sam, yes." The woman's voice sharpened. "Who is calling, please? I must have your name."

Oh, no, you mustn't, Cillay thought, and again hung up the receiver. Had she gained anything? R. S. Chellmand and Sam Chellmand were almost certainly one and the same. If that were so, there was something very odd about his being installed in the big bedroom upstairs. Why would a lawyer . . . with a home telephone listing of his own . . . move in here and pretend to be an insurance salesman? Or had someone else told her that part of it?

And whether or not R.S. and Sam were the same person, why should the woman at his home say he was out of town and the one at his office say he was not?

Uncertainty gnawed at her throughout the day. She was drawn to Sam Chellmand very strongly. Alan was pleasant, but he was only a college boy, while Sam was a man and a reassuringly competent one, she felt. A man who could be relied on. Except that she could not reconcile his being a lawyer with his hiding in Aunt Elsa's room and locking the door while he searched it. If it *had* been he behind that locked door.

He was not present for dinner, and Cillay missed him. Alan was there, and he followed her into the front hall afterward, the only place where they could

77

exchange a few words in private. He grinned at her rather shyly.

"I just wanted to ask . . . you can get loose from this place once in a while, can't you?"

"Get loose?" she repeated blankly.

"Oh, come on, you must have been asked for dates before," he protested, thinking she was being coy. "I thought maybe we could go out in the evening . . . there's a carnival starting tomorrow night, over on the square. Corny, kid stuff, but maybe it would be fun . . . if you'd go with me."

The thought of getting out of this depressing house . . . of actually laughing and having a good time . . . almost immobilized her. She had opened her mouth to accept when she remembered Pam.

"Oh! . . . but I couldn't leave my sister, really, though I'd love to go, otherwise. It's been such a long time since I went anywhere . . ." She stopped. "But I can't leave Pam alone."

His face showed disappointment. "Couldn't your aunt keep an eye on her for a few hours?"

But Aunt Elsa didn't like Pam, she thought. She didn't make remarks, the way Beatrice did, but she didn't like her. Cillay was sure of that. She shook her head with genuine regret. "I'm sorry. I don't see how I can do it."

The door had opened behind them and they both turned when Sam Chellmand spoke. "What's he trying to talk you into? Shall I throw him out on his ear?"

"Oh, no . . ."

"I thought she might enjoy going to the carnival tomorrow night," Alan said, shifting position on the hard stairs. "Only she says she can't leave her sister."

Chellmand surveyed them judicially for a moment. "Well, there's an easy solution to that, I should think. Take her sister along. Carnivals are geared for the six-year old mentality, I believe."

Hope leaped, for Cillay *did* want to go, and Alan's face brightened. "Well, yes, I suppose we *could* take her along, if she'd like to go."

"I'm sure she'd love to go, if you wouldn't mind having both of us . . ."

"OK, then," Alan agreed. "After dinner, around eight, OK?"

It was agreeable all around, and they all said their goodnights, Sam Chellmand with what seemed amused condescension. Cillay didn't mind his being amused; he had come up with a solution good enough to get her out for an evening of relaxation and fun.

She would have gone up the front stairs tonight, but Pam came wandering along the hall, looking for her.

"Why aren't you getting ready for bed, Pammy?"

"Beatrice said I could have some cocoa tonight, to help me sleep. Don't you want some too, Cillay?"

"Yes, I guess so. Although I don't really think I need anything to help me sleep except the chance to stop moving. Come on, let's go get it."

To her surprise, Beatrice was in the kitchen, hobbling about on her crutch; as they entered she began to pour out cocoa into a set of thick mugs, four of them.

"Isn't it hard for you to get around? I could have made it," Cillay exclaimed.

"Mrs. Pomeroy likes hers just so . . . quite sweet.

79

I didn't want to risk her annoyance by letting anyone else do it," Beatrice said with unwonted civility.
"You could get down the marshmallows, if you would
. . . they're up there. She likes lots of marshmallows
in her cocoa. I'm having mine with your aunt, but
you'll have to carry the tray for me; I can't manage
anything but this confounded crutch."

Cillay and Pam had fewer marshmallows than Mrs.
Pomeroy; even so, the cocoa was too sweet for Cillay's taste, and she left a little of it in the cup. "OK,
now, run up and start your bath. I'll be there as soon
as I've washed out our cups. And tomorrow I have
a surprise for you: Alan Creighton has asked us to go
to the carnival with him! Won't that be fun?"

Pam's lips shaped the word. "Carnival?"

"Where there will be a merry-go-round and ani-
mals in tents, perhaps, and cotton candy to eat . . ."

The girl's face lit up with delight. "A merry-go-
round? Can I ride it twice, Cillay? Can I?"

"We'll see. Now hurry and get ready for bed, and
I'll be up to tuck you in."

She had intended to get into bed early, herself, and
read one of the magazines Mrs. Sanding had lent her;
but by the time she'd arranged her pillows and the
light Cillay realized that she was too sleepy to read.
She felt very much as she had the first night in the
house, when she had laughingly wondered if Beatrice
had slipped something into their milk . . .

It was very still at the top of the house. Pam never
made any noise once she went to bed, and if anyone
was moving about on the floor below nothing could
be heard from here. Cillay lay quite still and fought
off a momentary wave of giddiness.

The cocoa tonight . . . it was the first time Beatrice had offered to do anything for them, on her own . . . it was a poor excuse, saying that Aunt Elsa might not like the cocoa if anyone else made it. Beatrice couldn't make anything else decently, so why cocoa?

Cillay spoke in a whisper. "My God! What if she did put something in it? That time, *and* this time?"

She remembered the dream she'd had that first night, a dream that someone was in the room with her, in the dark. But had it been a dream? The next morning the letter had been gone, the letter Aunt Elsa had written to her mother. The letter that should have been in her purse on the chair by the door. Easy to find, probably easy to extricate even in the dark, for it was the only letter in the handbag.

Why? Why on earth would Beatrice want to steal the letter? But, more frightening question yet, why had she wanted them drugged tonight?

For she had. Cillay was sure of it; already her mouth was beginning to feel dry, just as it had that other time, and her head swam slightly; not from fatigue, as she had thought, but *because she had been drugged*.

A small, strangled cry escaped from her throat. *What was Beatrice going to do while the girls on the third floor were sleeping so deeply? And how dangerous was it for Cillay and Pam?*

It occurred to her, somewhat tardily, that if she could throw up she might lessen the effect . . . but it was too late. Already her system was absorbing it, already she was past the point where she could control her body enough to get up and make it to the bathroom. Whatever Beatrice wanted, it would be quiet enough on the third floor.

Tears stung her eyes and she felt as if she were floating, as if her hands had gone away from her and were no longer under her control. Sam Chellmand had told her to come to him if anything frightened her . . .

But Sam Chellmand was down on the second floor, or perhaps not in the house at all, and she would be asleep long before she could reach him. She could not even get out of bed . . .

The light was still on, but she slept. Deeply, dragged down by whatever Beatrice had dissolved in the cocoa.

She slept.

Chapter 8

The alarm had been sounding for some time. Cillay came up out of the drugged sleep, struggling to orient herself. For a few more seconds she could not even reach out to turn off the alarm, the lethargy was so great.

Gradually it all came back to her. Her mouth was dry and she felt slightly unwell. Beatrice. Her mind strove to function again. Beatrice had put something into the cocoa last night. It had been served to Pam, also, and to Aunt Elsa. Had they all been drugged?

Moving was an effort, but she made it. Turn off the alarm. Stumble to the bathroom to wash her face in cold water . . . come winter, it was going to be unpleasant to be forever washing in cold water, but it took too long to wait for the hot water to climb this far up in the house.

Her head cleared somewhat with the shock of the cold water. By winter . . . by winter, she thought, I'd better have found some way to get out of here. Whatever Beatrice is doing, I don't want to be mixed up in it.

She opened Pam's door and looked in on her; the younger girl slept heavily, not stirring at the sound of the door. She wouldn't wake her, Cillay decided. If she came down late there was no one else in the kitchen to object to her being fed then. She wondered uneasily how much of the stuff Pam had gotten, and what it was. Pam had drained her cup, she remembered, and presumably taken more than Cillay had.

If Beatrice was plotting against Aunt Elsa in some way . . . at the moment she could not imagine what such a plot could consist of . . . her aunt should be warned. On the other hand, though, wasn't it possible . . . her mind skittered around the words . . . that Aunt Elsa and Beatrice were working together toward some secret purpose? For it was to Aunt Elsa that Beatrice had said, *We've got to do something about her, Pet! Maybe you're willing to take a chance, but I'm not! You can't be so stupid you don't see how dangerous it can be!*

She could, she supposed, take Sam Chellmand up on his offer of assistance, though she didn't exactly see what form that could reasonably take, either. Only how had he known something might happen to frighten her? How much did he know about what was going on in this house? And how trustworthy was a man who locked himself into other people's bedrooms while he ransacked them? Was he, in some way she could not fathom, involved himself in some nefarious scheme?

Her head ached, and she had no answers. She dressed and made her way down the back stairs . . . more carefully than before, feeling her way in the darker areas . . . suspicious of everything by this time. Including that broom that had been *"accidentally"* placed in the stairway rather than in the broom closet. Had it been put there deliberately in the hope that she would fall over it?

But it wouldn't have killed me, falling down a dozen steps, she thought. And why should it have benefited anyone to hurt me? Least of all Beatrice, the most likely suspect, whose duties she had taken over.

For a moment, thinking of Beatrice, she suspected that the woman had faked an injured ankle in order to get out of working; but almost immediately she recalled the way the ankle had swollen, so rapidly and so grossly. No, she hadn't faked that ankle.

The kitchen was empty, and there was no sign of anyone else stirring about the house. Cillay began, methodically, to get eggs out of the refrigerator and crack them into a big bowl. When she opened a drawer to get the egg beater, she stopped quite still.

Yesterday the drawer had been orderly; today it was chaos. Everything in it had been taken out, including the paper that lined the drawer, because it had been put back crookedly and the utensils dumped back in helter-skelter. And as she moved about the kitchen she found that virtually every drawer, every storage space, had been similarly searched.

Beatrice? Was this why she had wanted Pam and Cillay to sleep soundly? How much of the house had been torn apart this way? What was she searching for? Something not too large, judging by the areas that had been disturbed. Something no larger than, say, a shoe box. The same thing Sam Chellmand had been looking for yesterday? Could they be working together, looking for the same thing? They did not act as if they liked one another, but couldn't that be a cover?

No, she didn't think they were working together. More likely they were at cross purposes, but what purposes were they?

Beatrice was the last one at the table, making a commotion as she maneuvered into her chair and finally slid the crutch under it on the floor. She looked at Cillay quickly, then looked away.

"Your sister isn't here," Aunt Elsa stated flatly.

"No. She . . . she isn't feeling too well. Neither am I, as a matter of fact," Cillay said, carefully not glancing in Beatrice's direction. "I think we ate something that didn't agree with us. We both have sensitivities to some foods, and to drugs. Sleeping medications, things like that. They tend to make us have upset stomachs. I don't know what we could have gotten, but that's what it seems like."

"Oh, say, that's bad," old Mr. Gary said. "I've heard of people dying from doses of things that didn't agree with them. Allergic reactions, they call it."

"I guess we'll have to be more careful," Cillay said, unable to resist sliding an eye toward Beatrice, who was absorbed in her French toast. "I wouldn't want to get an overdose of anything." Would she take the hint that slipping sleeping medications to un-suspecting people might be dangerous? Or was it so broad that she would realize Cillay knew what she had done? Not until too late did it occur to Cillay that mentioning it at all might be further endangering herself and her sister.

"Sleeping pills can be most dangerous," Mrs. Fontana observed. "I always think one runs rather a risk to depend on such things. Outside of becoming addicted to them, I mean. It's so easy to take too much. But I suppose you didn't take any medicines, or you would know, so it must have been some food?"

"Yes, I suppose so." She wanted to suggest that

86

it might have been the cocoa, but if Beatrice harbored true malice toward them that might be very dangerous, indeed.

"I wonder," Mrs. Fontana said sweetly, turning to Mr. Gary, "if you would be so kind as to call me a cab, after breakfast? I am going to go into town. To my jewelers."

She said it with an innocent air that fooled no one, not even Cillay, who was quite caught up in her own problems. She was waiting for someone to ask the obvious question, and Aunt Elsa did.

"Your jewelers? You have your own jeweler, Mrs. Fontana?"

"Well, of course he isn't mine *exclusively*. But I have been doing business with him for many years. Would you believe that my wedding rings . . . the ones my last husband got for me . . . came from there, almost fifteen years ago?" She held out a hand, a poor scrawny, wrinkled thing, to display the impressive set of rings. "I'm going to consult with him about the possibility of resetting some other stones I have. The rings are so old fashioned, and this man does such beautiful work. I do think diamonds should be kept up to date, don't you?"

"Oh, by all means," Mrs. Sanding agreed enthusiastically. "I always have all my diamonds updated frequently." She wore a plain gold band as a momento of the late Mr. Sanding.

Miss Appleton tipped her blue head to one side, smiling roguishly at Mr. Gary. "I've never owned any diamonds . . . never had any desire to, really. I much prefer flowers, myself. Of course they aren't so valuable, and they don't last long . . . but then that makes it possible to have all the more of them, doesn't it? And they come in such lovely colors, and smell so nice . . . nobody can say that about a diamond."

"Well, I like flowers," Mrs. Fontana admitted. "But it's ever so nice to have a few diamonds around, too. One can convert them to cash so easily if one wants to, you know."

"Oh, yes, indeed," Mrs. Sanding said, and winked at Cillay quite openly.

"Well, I certainly hope we're both feeling well by tonight," Cillay said to the table at large, changing the subject. "Pam and I have been invited to go to a carnival, and we'd so much enjoy going."

"Invited . . . ?" Was Aunt Elsa's voice sharper than usual? "By whom?"

"Alan . . . Mr. Creighton. He's taking us both, after dinner."

"I remember the first time I ever went to a carnival," Mrs. Sanding said, leaning forward with a smile. "It was the first time I ever went anywhere with Mr. Sanding, and my, we had a marvelous time!"

They were off, all the old-timers, reminiscing. Cillay excused herself, hoping they wouldn't dally too long around the table. She didn't intend to work herself half to death today, especially since she still felt tired; she intended to enjoy this outing this evening, for it might be the only thing she would ever enjoy while she was in this house.

But before she began the breakfast dishes she sat down and wrote a short letter to a friend back in Serling. Monica Haines, whom she'd known all through school, was working now in a department store. Cillay wrote to ask about the chances of getting on there, and how much the job might pay, and if Monica would consider sharing her apartment for a few weeks while Cillay looked for work. She didn't know what she would do about Pam (she'd worry about that later), but she was afraid to stay on in this house.

Whatever Beatrice . . . and possibly Aunt Elsa . . . were mixed up in, Cillay wanted no part of it.

Dinner, she decided, would have to be simple enough to enable her to rest during the afternoon and also to clear up quickly afterward. She prepared the ingredients in advance for a gigantic chicken casserole and planned a salad to go with it, then went through her clothes to see what was suitable to wear to a carnival.

Surprisingly, nothing happened to prevent them from going, as Cillay had more than half expected would happen. At a quarter of eight they set out, on foot, for it was only six blocks to the square where the carnival was set up.

In mid-September the evening was mild and clear; the girls wore pleated skirts and sweater sets, Cillay's in orange, Pam's in blue, and Alan had discarded his usual sweatshirt and jeans for pressed slacks and a dressy sweater. Pam half-skipped along with them, openly anticipating. Cillay thought Alan might be rather uncomfortable about escorting both of them, but he didn't say anything. She suspected he was a very well brought up boy.

It was a typical tawdry carnival, but to Cillay it was a fairyland escape from prison. Bright lights, music, crowds of people milling about. Pam was entranced with everything, childlike in her inability to decide what she wanted to do first.

Alan seemed to be well supplied with cash; Cillay was relieved at that, for if his funds had been limited it might have been difficult to take two girls where he'd originally planned for only one.

They wandered along, looking at everything, eating popcorn and cotton candy. They were standing staring up at a monstrous contraption called the Sky Roller, trying to decide whether or not they were brave enough to ride it, when a familiar voice sent a delightful prickle of gooseflesh up Cillay's arms.

"Well, I wondered if I would run into you! Have you all gotten sick yet, eating junk?"

Sam Chellmand put out a hand to steady her when Cillay, turning, tripped over one of the electrical cables stretched across the grounds; the contact of his fingers was warm and strong, and she was pleased that he had come.

The same couldn't be said for Alan. His face darkened slightly, although he was courteous enough.

"You aren't going on that thing, are you?" Sam indicated the Sky Roller, which was turning its thrill seekers upside down, then dashing them at breakneck speed toward the ground, where they miraculously escaped death when it failed, by inches, to strike anything.

"Yes, let's!" Pam begged. "Let's, Cillay! I *like* being scared!"

Cillay felt a momentary tremor and thought, *I don't, not really being scared,* but Alan broke the spell.

"OK, let's go, then. We can all get in one of those things, I guess. Would you like to ride, too, sir?"

The "sir" was a deliberate attempt to relegate Sam Chellmand to another generation, but Sam only grinned and reached for his wallet. "Sure thing. Let me get these tickets. Alan, you can get the next ones."

Alan moved determinedly, isolating Cillay so that Sam and Pam were installed on one side of the gigantic bucket, he and Cillay on the other. The other couple waved and laughed at them, and Alan chuckled beside her as they strapped themselves in.

"I don't know what he's trying to do, but he's too old for you," he observed, checking to see that she had fastened her belt properly.

"He can't be more than twenty-eight or thirty," Cillay said without thinking, and earned Alan's frown.

"He's nearly old enough to be your father."

"Well, hardly. That's only eleven years older than I am, at the most. Oh, my, I hope this isn't going to make me sick!"

They were off, moving in dizzying arcs through the night sky, with the lights below them blending and blurring. In only partly assumed fear, she reached for Alan's hand, and he held tightly to hers during the entire ride, which restored him to good humor.

Pam, too, had enjoyed herself. She was breathless and laughing. All three of them enjoyed watching her delight in everything that went on. Sam put himself out to see that she was entertained, which was not at all difficult. Cillay's throat ached for a moment

91

as she thought how little pleasure there had been in her sister's life in the past year. And how little there was likely to be unless she succeeded in getting her away from Aunt Elsa's and establishing a home for her somewhere else.

And then, when they went on to the roller coaster, Alan suddenly found himself out-maneuvered. Sam handed Cillay into one of the coaches and got in beside her. There was nothing Alan could do but take the next one with Pam.

It was, Cillay realized, more exciting with Sam than it had been riding with Alan. Alan was a boy, like the brother she had never had, but Sam was a man. A handsome and exciting man.

They were half-way through the ride, their coach perched high on a peak overlooking the grounds, when something went wrong with the mechanism. The coach rattled to a stop.

"Now what?" Cillay leaned cautiously to look over the edge, drawing back when she saw how far down the ground was. "We won't be stuck up here, will we?"

"Not for long," Sam assured her. "You aren't scared, are you?"

She looked at him. It was nearly dark here, and they could make out no more than vague shapes in the coaches before and behind them, but she was close enough to see Sam's lean, dark face. "No," she said, and knew it was true. "I'm not afraid." She did not add that the reason was that he was there with her.

The men were swarming over the machinery below like ants on a dropped suckerstick, but she gave them no more thought. Sooner or later they would find the trouble and repair it. In the meantime, she was with the most attractive man she had ever known, and he was looking at her . . . It took her a few minutes to figure it out. The way a man looks at a girl he admires. No. *The way a man looks at a woman.*

She shivered, and he moved closer to her, putting an arm around her shoulders.

"Cold? We didn't really dress for being up so high, did we? The wind is chilly."

But it wasn't the cold, although she wouldn't have told him that. She liked the way his arm felt, warm and powerfully muscled.

"Cillay . . ."

She would never know what he'd intended to say, with his face so close to hers, his breath warm on her cheek, for at that moment the machinery roared to life below them and the coach began to move, slipping down the steep slope, faster and faster.

Instinctively, she ducked her head against his shoulder and he held it there, tightly, with one arm around her and his chin against her head. She had never felt this way before in her life, and she wished they might have gone on forever.

They did not, of course. She could see, when Sam helped her out onto the wooden platform, that Alan had observed at least the last part of that ride. He tried to erase the scowl from his face but wasn't totally successful.

"Wasn't it fun, Cillay!" Pam bubbled. "Weren't you *scared?*"

Cillay met Sam's eyes, briefly, warmly. "It was fun, wasn't it?"

"What do you want to do now?" Sam asked genially. "Anyone for trying his luck at pitching dimes? Shooting targets? Winning a teddy bear?"

They began to move along the midway, pausing to watch two men in a shooting contest at one of the booths. They separated a little, each maneuvering so as to be able to see. Pam wasn't interested in the shooting, only in the prizes. She chattered to Alan enthusiastically about the teddy bear, especially a big pink one.

"Go ahead," Sam suggested, amused. "Win it for her. You can shoot, can't you, Alan?"

"Yes, I can shoot." Alan dug into his pocket for change, dropped half a dollar on the counter, and accepted the rifle. "I'll get your teddy bear. That pink one, Mister. Save it for me."

Cillay watched, relaxed, warm, happy, even, for the first time in many months. She had needed this badly, this evening out with young people, laughing, talking . . .

There was shooting going on all around them, for there were several booths on the other side of the midway, too. So much shooting that no one noticed an extra shot, one not intended for the targets moving across the backs of the tents.

No one saw who fired a gun at Cillay.

Chapter 9

She felt a burning sensation and put up her hand to her cheek, drawing it away tinged with blood. She stared at it, incredulous, and made a small sound that brought Sam around on his heel, a shout of encouragement to Alan dying on his lips. He reached her side in two quick strides, putting up a hand to her face.

"What the hell . . . !"

"Hey . . . !" A man standing near was looking, too. "Hey, what's going on! She's been shot! This girl's been shot!"

Cillay stared at her bloodied fingertips, her lips parted, and felt herself sway. Sam cast an angry, unbelieving glance across the midway and moved immediately to put himself between the white faced girl and the shooting booth across the way.

"You all right, lady? Hey, this girl's been shot!"

The man fell back when Sam waved him away, but continued to stare.

It had only grazed her cheek; she knew that. But she was frightened, terribly frightened. Only Sam's hands on her arms kept her knees from buckling, as they threatened to do.

Alan turned away from the booth with a shout of triumph, holding aloft the giant teddy bear; his grin slid off his face in horror when he saw her.

"What happened? My God, what happened?"

"My teddy bear!" Pam crowed, and Alan let her take it out of his hands.

"Some crackpot shooting carelessly," Sam said angrily. "It's just a scratch, actually; does it hurt much?"

"Not yet," she said truthfully. "But it might have . . . it might have . . ."

She couldn't say the rest of the words, but she saw them echoed in Sam's eyes.

"I think that's it for tonight, kids. We'd better get on home."

Pam cried out in dismay. "But I haven't been on the merry-go-round yet! I can go on the merry-go-round, can't I, Cillay? You said I could!"

Sam brought out his handkerchief and held it to her cheek to check the bleeding. His hand was tense, hard.

Cillay lifted her eyes to his. "I did promise her, about the merry-go-round. I'm all right, I can wait that long."

Sam gave in, but reluctantly. "All right. One merry-go-round ride it is. Then we head for home."

Pam looked around at them, not understanding what was the matter; why was their evening of fun threatening to end so early? "*Two* rides?" she pleaded.

Sam had released his handkerchief so that Cillay held it herself. It was, truly, no more than a scratch on her cheek, and it wasn't bleeding profusely. "Let her, two rides," Cillay said.

Sam reached for his wallet but Alan made an angry gesture, perhaps compounded by his fright at Cillay's mishap. "No, this was supposed to be *my* date, I'll take care of it," he said. He peeled out a

96

bill and extended it to Pam. "There, ride until that's gone."

It was then, when a boy running down the narrow passageway jostled his arm, that Alan's wallet was knocked out of his hand, onto the littered ground. He made a grab for it, but a second boy pursuing the first accidentally kicked it and sent it rolling to Sam's feet. It was Sam who picked it up.

It was open, with a driver's license in view in one of the plastic windows; that was all Cillay saw. But as Sam started to hand it over to its owner she saw him pause, look at it sharply, then close it with a snap and smack it into Alan's outstretched palm. For a moment the two stared at one another; Alan looked strangely pale, although that might have been the effect of the madly colored lights around them. Sam was definitely grim.

Sam spoke without looking at her. "Go along with her, Cillay. See that she gets on and doesn't get lost when she gets off."

Cillay moved obediently, but her heart was thudding audibly. There was no need to put Pam on the merry-go-round; it would be safe enough to leave her in the line. There was a walled off area, she couldn't go anywhere else except onto the ride, and it would be the same way when she got off. She would be channeled right back out by this gate.

She gave Pam a little push, scarcely waiting to see that she had, indeed, joined the proper line, and then she moved around a concession stand, hoping that Alan and Sam were standing close enough to the far end of it so that she could overhear what they said.

They were. She paused at the corner, watching them through the windows of the cotton candy stand. They were engrossed with one another; she didn't think they would notice her there, for dozens of people were milling about, all laughing and talking.

Sam was angry, that was clear, while Alan appeared defiant.

"You damned young fool," Sam said clearly. "What are you trying to do?"

"I've got a right . . ." Alan began stiffly, but Sam's voice cut savagely through his words.

"Now, you listen to me! You move out of that house, tomorrow, and let me handle it! You understand?"

"How long have you been there?" Alan challenged. "How much have you found out?"

"That's beside the point," was Sam's crisp rejoinder. "If you haven't packed up and left by tomorrow night, I'll take steps to see that you're removed! Is that clear?"

Cillay edged closer to the glass, afraid she would miss part of the exchange, wondering what on earth this was all about.

"It's clear you don't want me around," Alan admitted, his own temper rising. "How much has it got to do with who I am and how much to do with Cillay?"

Sam stood quite still. "Cillay?"

"You think I didn't see the way you were holding her, back there on the roller coaster? This was supposed to be *our* date, and you horned in . . ."

"I thought," Sam said, dropping his voice so that

it was difficult to hear it, "that it might be wise to have someone tagging along. Just to keep an eye on things. Not that I did a hell of a lot of good, at that, if that shot wasn't an accident . . ."

"You don't think . . ." Alan's mouth dropped open in alarm. "It wasn't . . ."

"Who knows what it was? Who saw anything? It could have been an accident, it probably was. But as soon as that kid gets off the merry-go-round get them home, understand? And start throwing your stuff in your suitcase, and go on home."

"I don't have to do what you say, Mr. Chell-mand . . ."

"You stay here past tomorrow night and you'll see about that, Alan my lad. Come on, let's get the girls; they've been out of sight long enough. There may be another sharpshooter around, one with better aim."

She had to move quickly to reach the exit gate ahead of them. Her head had begun to ache and she was shaking; whether in delayed reaction to the shot that had grazed her cheek or to the conversation she had just heard she couldn't have said. She couldn't even fake surprise when they materialized beside her, but they were both too tense to notice.

"She's just started around for the third time. She had enough money to go once more."

Alan said nothing. Sam merely nodded. They flanked her, almost as if they were a body guard.

She tried to make her mind function. Sam had suggested that someone had deliberately shot at her, that it might not have been some careless amateur with a target gun. Deliberately shot at her . . . not,

99

it stood to reason, with the idea of scratching her face. Had it been an inch to the right . . . she shuddered.

Why? What possible reason could anyone have for wanting to harm her? The only people she knew were those who were members of her aunt's household. And what was the meaning of that angry exchange between the two men? It seemed to suggest that they were both in Elsa Pomeroy's household for a specific purpose, and that there was danger involved in it somehow.

It was all incredible, like something seen in a bad movie, but the stinging crease in her cheek proved it was not imaginary.

Who could possibly have attempted to shoot her? Beatrice? Beatrice was the only one who had demonstrated open animosity. But Beatrice was crippled; she didn't move at all without her crutch and couldn't have hoped to mingle unobtrusively with a crowd or to get away in a hurry. She couldn't have walked this far from the house, either, and she had no car. Would anyone dare take a taxi to the scene of a prospective murder, and then have it wait until the deed was done so that she could ride home again?

A giggle, slightly hysterical, rose in her throat. Surely Beatrice couldn't have managed it, taxi or no.

Aunt Elsa?

Her brief burst of amusement dissolved. How terrible, to suspect her own aunt of something like this. But she, too, seemed automatically ruled out, for much the same reasons. Her bulk was as incapacitating as Beatrice's injured foot. And the situation, taxi-wise, was the same. Besides, her aunt had invited her to come here. Why should she now want to be rid of her badly enough to shoot at her?

The only thing she could be sure of was that neither Alan nor Sam Chellmand had had a hand in it. They had both been standing within a few feet of her at the time the shot was fired.

Cillay was tempted to try to talk to Sam, to implore him to tell her what was going on, even to ask for his help if she didn't get a favorable reply from Monica about the possibility of a job in Serling. Yet there was just enough doubt in her mind to make her hesitate.

Sam was in the house under false pretenses. He was a lawyer, but what did that prove? There were crooked lawyers, as well as crooked bank clerks. It seemed fairly clear that his interests were not the same as Aunt Elsa's, and to whom did she owe her loyalty?

And where, in heaven's name, did Alan Creighton come into the picture? What had Sam seen in his wallet that had sent him into such a cold rage?

She probably couldn't pry any information out of Sam, she concluded, but she just might be able to get somewhere with Alan. She decided, to begin with, she would try.

"She's finally off the damned thing," Sam said a few inches from her ear. "Let's get out of here."

Pam came through the crowd toward them, her face shining with happiness, clutching the pink teddy bear to her chest. At least she had had a marvelous evening, Cillay thought, and saw that the sullen expression had faded from Alan's face, too, at the sight of her.

"Oh, it was such fun! Are we going home now?"

"Yes, dear, we are. And you'll thank Alan and Mr. Chellmand for giving us a good time, won't you?"

"Oh, yes!" Pam agreed, doing so with her own small-girl charm.

They had begun to move toward the exit gate, and Cillay saw that Sam was looking at her rather quizzically. "So Alan's *Alan* and I'm *Mr. Chellmand*, am I?"

"Well, you're rather . . . older. It seems sort of discourteous of a child to call you by your first name."

"My grandfather is *Mr. Chellmand*," he told her, smiling faintly, "and as you are *not* a child you may call me Sam, if you please."

"All right," Cillay agreed, smiling, and was rewarded by a scowl from Alan when she was caught at it. She widened her smile in his direction until he relented, for it was Alan she wanted to trick out of some information . . .

Her cheek had stopped bleeding and did not hurt badly; it was, after all, an extremely minor injury. Alan made a pointed move to drop behind to walk with her, and Sam amiably joined Pam ahead as they left the carnival grounds and began the walk toward home.

"It was very nice, Alan, and I'm so glad you asked us. Pam is delighted with her teddy bear."

"I'd rather have won one for you," he said gruffly.

"But I'm just as happy that she has it. Really I am."

"You're . . . you're a very nice girl, Cillay. Do you know that?"

She laughed. "Why? Because I like my sister

102

and enjoy seeing her have fun? She hasn't had much, lately, and I don't have time to entertain her any more."

"It's a crime the way your aunt makes you work. Like you were a slave or something," Alan said.

"Oh, it isn't all that bad. And Beatrice will be able to get around again pretty soon, so it isn't forever."

"What'll you bet Beatrice will find some way to leave you with most of it," Alan predicted shrewdly. "Beatrice just isn't the domestic type."

"No, she isn't, is she? I wonder how she ever got into such a position, when she doesn't like cooking or keeping house? I mean, she can't be over thirty or thirty-five, do you think? And there must be lots of other things she could do besides help run a boarding house."

They moved through the quiet streets, where the mists again hung about the street lights and most of the houses were already dark, but tonight Cillay was not afraid. Not with Sam and Alan along.

It was only when they were mounting the front steps of Aunt Elsa's house that her bubble of pleasure burst. How long would it take to hear from Monica, and if the reply were in the affirmative how would she tell her aunt what she had decided to do?

She knew, the moment she opened the door into her room, that someone . . . Beatrice? . . . had been here while she was gone. Like the kitchen, the room had been thoroughly and methodically searched.

Chapter 10

Everything was slightly out of order. Her drawers, not ordinarily so neat, but having just been so as she had so recently put her things into them, were disarranged. Things had been moved about in the closet. Her suitcases, now stacked on a shelf at the top of the closet, had been taken down and put back in a different order.

The same situation existed with regard to Pam's room. A picture had been shifted and now hung crookedly. The bed had been moved . . . there were marks on the thin carpeting . . . so that the rug itself could be turned back? That's what it looked like. What on earth was missing or hidden? And who was looking for it? This was a laborious climb for either Beatrice or Aunt Elsa; in fact, she was nearly positive that Mrs. Pomeroy, at least, simply could not have made it. She got out of breath and had palpitations climbing the half dozen steps that led to the back yard.

How long had it been after she and Pam had left with Alan before they'd met Sam at the carnival grounds? Had *he* had time to do all this?

He might have, she conceded, if he'd been fast, and she thought Sam would have been. And she was reasonably certain he had searched the kitchen, the morning she'd fallen down the stairs. She remembered her compunction about looking around his room.

She had a sudden, unwelcome thought: could *Sam* have put the broom on the stairs? Not to cause her to break her neck, but to give him warning that she was coming, knowing she would be the first one stirring?

But no, if he'd done that he need only have gotten away when she did fall; he wouldn't have given himself away by opening the door to see if she were all right. She wouldn't have known he was in that part of the house where he didn't belong if he hadn't done that.

There had been no opportunity to talk to Alan tonight; they had all come into the house together and up as far as the second floor. If Alan had seen to it that she didn't linger to talk to Sam, Sam had also delayed entering his own room until assured that she was going on immediately to the third floor.

The top floor was isolated and lonely. There had been no cocoa tonight, nothing eaten all day that she hadn't prepared for herself. She could prop chairs under the door knobs, leaving open the passageway through the bathroom so that Pam could reach her if necessary, and she would be perfectly safe, she thought.

But she could not go to sleep. She could not even bring herself to get into bed and turn off the light. She paced the floor, wishing she had the nerve to go down and talk to Sam alone. But she wasn't sure of him. She wanted to be, but she wasn't.

If only she knew whether Aunt Elsa were an innocent victim of whatever Beatrice (and/or Sam?) was up to, or a sly conspirator!

There was no one to tell her. She was acutely aware

of how alone she was, how completely on her own. If only Pam were a normal sister they could discuss it, make a decision together. Only poor Pam could not help in any way; she could never be more than an added liability, Cillay thought, and then was ashamed.

The house creaked in an alarming fashion, and she froze, facing her door, wondering if it were only the old house complaining as its ancient timbers cooled or if there were someone out there. Beatrice had drugged her before when she came up here; surely she wouldn't come otherwise.

Soft sounds . . . rustlings, murmurings . . . her tension grew until she couldn't bear it any longer. Cillay walked to the door and flung it open.

Light spilled across the bare varnished boards of the hallway. The entry to the stairs was a gaping black void. There was nothing moving. It was only her imagination, added to the natural creakings of an old house, that had led her to believe otherwise.

There was no relief in the knowledge. For she hadn't imagined the other things that had happened since she'd come here. She stood in the doorway, casting a shadow into the hallway. It stretched far out . . . Cillay took a step forward. The hall was a long one, stretching from back to front of the house; its far end was lost in darkness, for there were no bulbs in the light fixtures out there. It was lined on both sides by closed varnished doors. She had never ventured to look into any of the other rooms, for Beatrice had said they were all empty. But she was sure all of the doors had been closed every time she had come through this end of the corridor.

Tonight one door was ajar. She could see the darker line along one side of it.

Had Beatrice (whoever?) been in the other rooms up here, too?

She listened carefully, but so far as she could tell the household was asleep. And neither Beatrice with her crutch nor Aunt Elsa with her fat could climb those stairs noiselessly; this last flight was uncarpeted and any shoe would announce its presence.

Cillay took a breath, pushed her own door wider to let out the maximum amount of light, and moved toward the unlatched door.

Her fingers touched it lightly, and it moved with a protesting creak of unoiled hinges. She felt along the wall . . . would there be good bulbs here? . . . and the room sprang into relief under a forty watt bulb.

Cillay drew in a breath and held it.

The room was furnished similarly to the ones in which she and Pam slept. Odd pieces of old fashioned furniture, a worn rug. And this room, too, had been searched, by someone who had made no effort to cover up his actions. The bed had been stripped and the bedding left in a heap on the floor. The mattress was turned back, one corner still caught on the head of the bed. Drawers had been pulled out of the dresser and overturned, left in an angry stack on the floor. A picture, covered with glass, had been thrown to the floor and smashed as if in a fit of rage.

Whatever the searcher had sought, he had not found it. She was sure of that. The entire room bespoke frustrated fury.

Cillay turned off the light and closed the door. Then, quite methodically, she progressed down the entire length of the hallway, turning on lights and looking in on similar scenes of devastation.

Whoever had done this had done it recently. Assuredly since Cillay and Pam had come, probably within the last day or so, for there was as yet no dust on the surfaces wiped clean by the blankets and pillows flung about. If it had been done tonight Sam Chellmand could not have done it, for there simply hadn't been time. And if someone else had followed her to the carnival with the intention of shooting her, that person hadn't had time to do it, either.

Last night, when she had been sleeping soundly after that sickeningly sweet cocoa? Or the first night, when Beatrice had so generously poured out tall glasses of milk for them? She had done it with her back turned to them; could she have put something into the glasses without being detected? There was no question in Cillay's mind that she not only could have, but had in fact done so.

Every room on the third floor, with the exception of her own and Pam's, had been literally torn apart. In one room a great strip of wallpaper had been torn from the wall, and kicked into a heap. In another a china figure . . . it was difficult to tell now what it had been . . . had been pulverized underfoot.

And, in the end, Cillay returned to her room no wiser than she had been before. Someone had been searching every possible hiding place for something . . . and upon failing to do so had vented wrath and violence upon what was there. She still knew nothing about what the missing or hidden object could be, and could only guess as to the perpetrator of the damage.

She did, at last, prop chairs under the door knobs, check on her sister, and crawl into bed and turn out the light. She did, at last, fall asleep and dream.

The first spate of dreams was again frightening . . . a gigantic black widow spider, sucking chocolates, this time reaching out with a razor-sharp thrust of a leg to leave a shallow incision across her cheek . . . Beatrice, standing over her with an exaggeratedly hooked nose, forcing her to drink a mug of drugged cocoa, while Pam already lay seemingly dead on the floor . . . and then she was in her own room . . . not *this* one, but the one at home, back in Serling . . . and all its walls had been slashed with knives and the stuffing hung out of all the mattresses and upholstery . . .

She woke, and shivered, and tried to think of something pleasant to prevent the return of the bad dreams. Sitting on the roller coaster, at the top of the track, with Sam Chellmand's arm around her. Plunging down the incline with her head buried against him, his strength holding her. At last she smiled faintly, and again fell asleep.

She was up earlier than usual, for she wanted to talk to Alan before he left the house. He nearly got away from her, as she hadn't heard him come down, and he had already opened the front door when she called.

"Alan . . . you'll be here for dinner tonight, won't you?"

"Sure." Remembering Sam's orders of last night, his forehead furrowed momentarily, but he had made up his mind to ignore Sam, she suspected. "I don't have any late classes today, so I'll be home around three, probably. Maybe we could take a walk or something . . ."

"With Pam? Over to the park, maybe?" Cillay suggested. "We could talk while she plays on the swings."

"OK. It's a date," Alan agreed. "I'll see you then."

He was a nice boy, she thought, returning to the kitchen. And she thought he'd tell her what was going on if she asked him. She could offer to pool information with him, if she had to; not that she had reached any conclusions of any value, but she knew of some odd happenings that were probably unknown to Alan. She did not, as usual, see Sam at all that morning. He apparently was up and out very early and never ate breakfast here. She wanted to talk to him, too, but not with any hope of prying information out of him. She had no confidence in her ability to do that.

She considered what to say when the lodgers asked about the scratch on her cheek, as she was sure they would do. At first she had thought to say she'd simply scraped it on something. But if someone in this house were responsible for it . . . as Sam had intimated might be the case . . . to do that would be to reveal that she knew there was something significant about it, that she knew it was not an accident.

So, when Mrs. Sanding inquired solicitously, she admitted that someone had shot carelessly at the carnival last night.

"I never heard of such a thing! I hope you told him what you thought of such stupidity!"

"No. I didn't see who did it, and there was no way to find out. There were three booths, I think, with

110

shooting galleries, and as I wasn't actually hurt it didn't seem worthwhile to make a fuss about it."

"But it spoiled your evening," Mrs. Fontana said regretfully in her soft voice.

"Oh, no, not really. Pam had a lovely time . . . didn't you, darling? . . . and it was fun to watch her. Alan won a teddy bear for her. And we all laughed a lot . . ."

"Mr. Chellmand hugged Cillay on the roller coaster," Pam put in, giggling. "Alan didn't like it."

"Mr. Chellmand?" Mrs. Pomeroy paused with her spoon half-way to her mouth. "Was he there? I thought your date was with Alan Creighton?"

Too late, Cillay realized she ought to have cautioned Pam not to mention Sam, for it might seem quite out of character for this usually taciturn older man to have joined a group of adolescents at a carnival. Whatever his purpose in being in this house, she was in no hurry to expose him as anything but another roomer.

"Oh, he happened along after we'd been there for a while, and walked around with us for a time," she said casually.

"It sounds," said Mrs. Pomeroy, around a mouthful of oatmeal and brown sugar, "as if Mr. Chellmand was taking liberties."

"Oh, no, not at all! You know how it is on the roller coaster . . . you scream and hold onto whoever you're with. That was all it was. Pam, would you pass the sugar, please?"

And they were safely diverted from the topic of Mr. Chellmand.

Mrs. Fontana brought up another subject of considerably more interest. "I suppose I've only mislaid it," she began, looking around the table, "because I can't believe anyone here would have taken it, but one of my rings is missing. You'll remember it, the one with the large diamond surrounded by tiny emeralds. I'd had it reset, and it was quite lovely. I left it on my dresser last evening, but this morning it wasn't there. I'm almost certain I left it on my dresser."

"Sounds too valuable to leave lying about like a hair pin," Mrs. Sanding commented tartly. "Don't you have a box or something to keep your diamonds in, so they won't tarnish?"

Miss Appleton pounced on that. "Diamonds don't tarnish, my dear. Didn't you know that?"

"No sense of humor," Mrs. Sanding muttered. "And how would I know anything about diamonds? *I* never had any."

"You must have misremembered where you put it," Mrs. Pomeroy declared positively. "No one in this house would have taken it, I'm sure."

"Well, that's what I thought, only I'm *sure* I remember it being there before I went to bed, and it wasn't there when I came back from the bathroom this morning."

"Perhaps you laid it on the side of the sink," Mrs. Sanding suggested hopefully, "and it's fallen into the drain. We could send for the plumber and have him tear the pipes apart . . ."

"I did not take the ring into the bathroom," Mrs. Fontana assured her. "One does *not* wash one's hands wearing diamonds, my dear. I *always* remove my rings before going into the bathroom."

112

"It might have fallen down the register, then. It would be small enough to fit through the grillwork."

"It was on the *dresser*," Mrs. Fontana insisted. "And it's quite valuable . . . I left my door open, and anyone might have seen it there . . ."

"Now you're suggesting that one of us is a thief," Mrs. Sanding said crossly. "Well, I didn't take it. I've gotten along nicely for seventy-two years without any jewels, so why would I steal some to be buried in?"

"Are you counting on being buried soon?" Miss Appleton asked, her voice sweet.

"Well, we can't *all* live to be eighty," Mrs. Sanding said, and smiled in gratification at having brought a faint flush to Elizabeth Appleton's cheeks.

"I wouldn't want to call in the police," Mrs. Fontana was saying earnestly, "such unpleasant people, the police, don't you think? But one can't ignore the disappearance of a twelve hundred dollar ring, can one?"

"Twelve hundred dollars?" Adam Gary echoed. "That's a lot of ring, at that!"

"I'm sure we'll find it. You won't do anything hasty, Mrs. Fontana," Aunt Elsa said positively, "until we've had a chance to clean your room thoroughly, of course. It may well have fallen into a crack somewhere, or onto the floor."

"But Cillay just cleaned my room and she won't be doing it again until next week."

"It is to be hoped," Mrs. Sanding said, *sotto voce*, "that one's knees will bend to enable one to get down and look under one's bed."

"I'll be happy to go up and help you look for it," Cillay volunteered, feeling that Mrs. Sanding was going to say something soon so sufficiently out-rageous that breakfast would end in a hair-pulling match. "As soon as I've finished in the kitchen this morning. Will that be all right?"

Mrs. Fontana gave her a sweet and rather vague smile. "Thank you, my dear. That would be very kind of you."

The ring was, in fact, quite easy to find. So easy that Cillay wondered uncomfortably how Mrs. Fontana herself could have missed it. It was on the floor just under the edge of the ornate old dresser.

Mrs. Fontana was effusive in her thanks, and immediately went down in triumph to show it off to everyone. Cillay followed more slowly. Had someone seen the ring on the dresser and taken it? And then, alarmed at the threat of the police being called in, put it back while Mrs. Fontana was not there? An idiot could have found it where it was, and Mrs. Fontana was not an idiot, although she was certainly somewhat careless with her belongings.

Cillay went back to the kitchen to decide what to have for lunch, her thoughts swinging from Mrs. Fontana's ring to her coming talk with Alan. Surely, she thought, her spirits rising at the prospect of being away from the house for an hour or two, with another young person instead of all these old ladies, she would find out something then; Alan would be persuaded to share his secrets . . . or enough of them to help her come to a decision about what to do.

The trouble was, Alan did not come back.

Chapter 11

She waited for him until well after five. At first she thought he'd simply been delayed at school, or missed a bus. And then, as time passed, she began to grow concerned.

There was nothing she could think of to do. It was time to attend to dinner preparations, but she left the kitchen door open and even posted Pam in the front parlor with her drawing materials, telling her to report when Alan came in.

It was time to put the meal on the table, and he had not arrived. She was disappointed, but she was increasingly alarmed, as well. Alan, she knew, had looked forward to spending some time with her. He knew the telephone number, and if he'd been delayed in some legitimate fashion he ought to have called. It was evident that he was well brought up and would have been taught to call if unable to keep an engagement. That he had not done so suggested to Cillay that for some reason he was unable to call. In the light of her peculiar accident the previous night, this was disturbing.

But he left here in daylight, she thought, carrying food to the table. He went to school, on the city bus, as usual. What could possibly have happened to him between here and the college?

Sam was not there for dinner, but when he did come in around seven o'clock Cillay, after a surreptitious glance around to make sure she was unobserved, followed him up the stairs.

"Mr. Chellmand . . . Sam . . . please . . . !"

He stopped in the upper hallway, smiling a little in welcome. His face was extremely pleasant when he was smiling. "How do you still have the energy to run upstairs after the day you've put in? Isn't her majesty Queen Beatrice off that crutch yet to help you?"

"Sam . . . something's happened to Alan!"

"To Alan?" His smile vanished. "What makes you think so?"

"He hasn't come home. He left this morning as usual, but he hasn't come back . . ."

His facial muscles relaxed. "Oh, is that all. Well, I suspect he'd just tired of this moth-eaten old firetrap and gone home . . . this was a most unlikely place for a college student to stay, you know. Or he's found a more convenient place, closer to the campus. He was wasting an hour a day on the buses."

"No, you don't understand. We'd made a date . . . sort of . . . we were going to take Pam to the park this afternoon. He didn't have any late classes and he said he'd be back around three. But he never came and he never called. Something *must* have happened to him."

His mouth softened as he looked down on her. "Poor baby . . . I don't suppose it's happened to you before, has it? Being stood up? I shouldn't think it would . . . you're a lovely little girl . . . but it *does* happen, you know. He'll probably drop you a note in a day or two, or maybe call . . . but you

116

wait and see. He's simply moved out into a better place."

She was stung by his words. Poor baby . . . being stood up . . . little girl. She backed away from him, indignation sparkling in her eyes.

"You wanted him to go, didn't you? Just as you told me to go. But he didn't! I know he intended to come back here this afternoon the same as always! Can't we do something to find out?"

"What do you suggest we do? Call in the police?"

Her breast heaved angrily, impotently. "Well, yes, if we can't find out any other way. There has to be a *reason* why he didn't come home."

"There undoubtedly is. And when the police run him down to ask him he's going to be embarrassed and annoyed. Are you willing to risk that?"

"Yes. If there's any chance something *has* happened to him."

"Hmmm. Stubborn as well as beautiful, are you?" His compliment, coming as it did after goodnatured derision, fell flat. "Well, I'll tell you what. Let's take a look in his room and make sure he hasn't cleared it out, first, shall we? I mean, no sense in making fools of ourselves. If his stuff is all still here, we'll know he hasn't moved out. All right?"

It seemed reasonable to look. She led the way, knowing she was right, that Alan hadn't simply packed and left without saying goodbye, without canceling their date or making another one . . .

And stopped on the threshold of Alan's room.

The bed was neatly made. There were no personal items to be seen anywhere. Sam threw open the closet

117

door to reveal nothing but a collection of wire hangers that jangled in the draft he had created. He opened the dresser drawers, and there was nothing in them. No suitcase, no school books. Nothing at all to show that Alan Creighton . . . or anyone else . . . had ever lived in this room.

Her face was white.

"I don't believe it. He said he was coming back this afternoon, and he meant to do it."

"Dear Cillay," Sam said gently, placing his hands on her shoulders and looking into her face. "Don't you think I would be concerned if I thought anything could have happened to that boy? It hasn't. He's simply packed up and left, gone home or to another room somewhere. I know it's a blow to your pride, but you'll get over that. Were you really so attached to him? He's only a boy . . ."

Cillay jerked away from his hands. "My pride has nothing to do with it. And I'm not . . . not infatuated with him, or anything so foolish as that! I simply *cannot* believe that he would move out without so much as saying goodbye to me!"

Sam said nothing, but his sympathetic expression was infuriating.

"When did he do it?" Cillay demanded. "He left for school this morning . . . I saw him go out of the house! He was carrying his school books, and that's all! No suitcases, nothing else!"

"This is a big house, and you can't watch every door all the time. He could have been in and out any number of times and no one the wiser." How much did Sam Chellmand know about being able to do that, she wondered angrily. "Give it up, Cillay. Wait a day

118

or two . . . I'll bet he'll call you, or send you a note. Wait and see."

He was pacifying her as if she were a spoiled, unreasonable child. Tears scalded her eyes and she turned away so that he would not see them.

"All right. I thought you'd help me, but if you won't, I'll call the police myself . . ."

"No." His voice had changed completely. It was lower, colder, and most compelling. "No, don't call the police. You can do nothing but harm by such an action, believe me."

"Why should I believe you?" she flung at him. "You make cryptic remarks and don't explain them, you ridicule my genuine concern for a friend, and now you presume to give me orders . . . !" She waited for him to deny it, but he did not.

"I now presume to give you orders," he confirmed in the same quiet voice. "You will not call the police, do you understand that perfectly? There are reasons why this would be very stupid, and I cannot explain them now, but I expect you to take my word for it."

"Why should I take your word for anything?" A perceptive man would have heard the cry for help in her voice; perhaps he did, for he reached for her again, and this time his hands were not so rough.

"Because I ask you to," he said, and quite without warning bent his head and kissed her.

It was, literally, her first grown up kiss. Not that she'd never kissed a boy at all, but they had all been *boys* . . .

Sam's body was hard against hers, his arms firm, his kiss compelling, and she had the sudden firm conviction that no one else would ever stir her as Sam did.

"You will not call the police . . . or anyone else. Will you?" he asked quietly, releasing her.

She did not, at the moment, think she would; but she was too stubborn to give in completely and she retained enough sense to realize that, given a little time and a little distance from Sam, she might eventually feel quite differently about it.

"I don't know," she said honestly, and Sam's smile lighted his greenish eyes as well as his mouth.

"*I* know. I trust *you*, Cillay, whether you can trust me or not. Now you'd better get out of here before the Amazon finds us kissing in hallways and reports us to the formidable Mrs. Pomeroy."

With that he was gone, leaving her there in the corridor, alternating between delight and dismay, between heat and cold.

She still did not believe Alan had simply packed up and walked out, but she didn't know what she could do about it. And she suspected that if she were wise she would stay away from Sam Chellmand . . . he was one of those men her mother had told her about, who can charm a woman into doing anything he wants her to do.

"So easily," she breathed in a whisper. "Just by looking at me . . . no, by *touching* me. I must not let him touch me any more."

The resolution was made easily enough. Keeping it might be something else again, especially when she remembered how it had felt, to be in Sam's arms.

There was no word from Alan by morning. All through breakfast Cillay worried about him, and finally could keep still no longer.

"Aunt Elsa . . . did Alan say anything to you about leaving?"

"Leaving?" Elsa Pomeroy helped herself to another serving of jam on her toast. "No. His rent is due to-day, however; I suppose we won't collect if he is leaving. I do think it would have been courteous to give us some notice if he intended to leave. He has had one of the more desirable rooms."

Beatrice's voice carried a razor-edge. "Is he leaving? Or has he gone already?"

"He seems to have gone," Cillay admitted wretchedly.

"*Seems* to have gone? He's either gone or he hasn't," Mrs. Pomeroy stated. "Which is it?"

"His things are gone from his room."

"Well, then, he's gone. Without so much as a by-your-leave. Young people today, that's all you can expect of them. No gratitude, no consideration for other people. You'd better change his bed, ready the room for someone else."

No one cared where Alan had gone, or why, or under what circumstances. No one but herself.

Sam, no doubt, thought Alan had gone because Sam had told him to go, had even, in a way, threatened him if he did not. But Cillay did not believe this had frightened him off. Alan might not like to admit he'd been driven off, if he had been, but he wouldn't have made arrangements to meet her later in the day if he hadn't intended to do it. She was sure of that.

While she washed dishes she tried to think of some way to check on him. If he'd left of his own accord, fine. But what if he hadn't? What if something had happened to him and no one was so much as looking for him?

She had no idea where his family lived. She didn't know any of his friends. But if he were all right he must have gone to school as usual this morning . . .

Of course! City University! Someone there could undoubtedly tell her if he had turned up for classes.

She didn't want to try to call from the house, for there was only the rather public front hall instead of a phone booth, and she was certain to be overheard. But there was a pay phone on the street near the market, and this was her day to shop. She determined to call the college from there.

It was dismaying, when she looked up the City University number in the phone book, to discover that there was not one number but something like fifty. Cillay stared at the full column of numbers; where could she start? Calling them all would take more dimes than she possessed, and would probably be a waste of time in the bargain. Registrar's office? Would that be a logical place to start?

The girl who answered was polite but incredulous at her request. "I don't think you understand, miss. We have over ten thousand students! It would be impossible to locate one student, especially with no more information than you've given me! Most of the classes don't even take roll! I don't see any way to help you. If this is an emergency, perhaps the police . . ."

"Wouldn't it be possible for you to check and see that you have a student named Alan Creighton registered?" Cillay asked desperately. "If you could give me his home address . . . so I could get in touch with his parents . . ."

"I'm sorry, I'm not allowed to give out that sort of information."

"But I'm afraid something has happened to him, and I don't know how else to find out . . ." Did the hint of tears in her voice communicate itself to the girl on the other end of the line?

"Well, I suppose there'd be no harm in verifying the fact that we have such a student. And while I can't give out his address, I guess if it's really an emergency I could call his home and leave a message for *him* to call *you* . . . if that would help you any. If it's a local call, that is."

"Oh, yes, would you do that?" She waited while the girl went to look up Alan's address, feeling weak-kneed in relief. For if Alan had moved his family would know where. And if they did, then he was all right.

But the girl's voice, when she came back on the line, was not encouraging. "Would you mind spelling that for me again? C-R-E-I-G-H-T-O-N? That's what I had written down. But we have no student by the name of Alan Creighton. In fact, we haven't anyone at all by the name of Creighton."

Their conversation was prolonged for several more minutes, but there was nothing more the girl could do. Perhaps he was enrolled at the junior college . . . but he had worn a sweat shirt saying City University on it . . .

Cillay finally gave up, succumbing briefly to the tears that flooded her eyes. Well, she might have expected it, at that. For Sam had seen something in

Alan's wallet . . . a driver's license in another name, a name Sam recognized, she thought. And if Alan had given a false name at the rooming house there was no way of tracing him at all.

Except through Sam. Sam knew what that name was. Only how to persuade him to investigate?

Mrs. Sanding greeted her brightly when she got back to the house, waving an envelope at her.

"Letter for you! Mailman came just a few minutes ago!"

Cillay lowered her bag of groceries onto the table at the foot of the stairs and reached for it eagerly. Alan had written, after all . . .

Only he hadn't. The letter was postmarked Serling, Illinois. A reply to her letter to Monica.

"From a beau?" Mrs. Sanding asked slyly, but Cillay shook her head. "No, a girl friend. Thank you, Mrs. Sanding."

She and Pam carried the groceries back to the kitchen and put them away, and then she opened the letter. It was short but friendly . . . heartwarmingly friendly.

"I've got a couch that opens into a double bed," Monica had written. "I can't guarantee a job where I am, but they are hiring a few inexperienced girls to train for Christmas saleswork. At any rate, come and we'll find you something, and so what if it takes a month or two? We'll make out, and Daddy is always good for a loan if that should be necessary. It will be great to see you again; we used to have such a lot of fun before your mother got sick and everything. Let me know when you're getting in and I'll meet you . . .

I've even got a car of sorts!" It was signed, "Love, Monica."

Again tears stung her eyes, but Cillay blinked them away. She would go, she decided. Before she left she would try to talk Sam into determining where Alan was, not because she was hurt that he'd stood her up but to be certain he really was all right. And then she would tell Aunt Elsa that her friend had found her a job, and it would be better if she returned to Serling.

But again it was easier to make a decision than it was to carry it through. For when Cillay went to count her money, estimating how much it would take to get them home and how long it would last, paying just for their food until she found a job . . . it was gone. The entire one hundred and twenty dollars. The silver in her coin purse was untouched . . . seventy-two cents there. But there were no bills at all.

It had been frightening to know that someone did not want her in this house. It was even more frightening to realize now that someone did not intend that she should be able to leave it.

Chapter 12

To Cillay's extreme frustration, Sam did not return for dinner nor, so far as she could determine, was he home at ten that evening when she was ready to go up to bed.

It was more than Alan's disappearance, now. She was thoroughly scared to stay on in this house, afraid for herself and Pam; she only realized how bad it was when she found that someone had stolen her money and removed her only means of escape.

Sam had told her that if she were frightened she could go to him. Well, she was frankly terrified . . . and she would talk to him. His position in this house was something of a mystery, but he didn't frighten her nearly so much as Beatrice did . . . or, she felt guilty thinking it, for she was her father's own sister . . . Aunt Elsa. She was in over her head. She had to have some help to escape from this place.

Maybe it would be possible for her to get a night job . . . yes, why hadn't she thought of that before? In a restaurant, perhaps, as a waitress . . . so that she could leave Pam asleep at night, and be there with her during the day. Something could be worked out, there must be some way to do it. If only she could get away from this house.

Sam always left the house early in the morning, usually before anyone else was up. She couldn't bear the thought of waiting another full day to speak to him; her nerves weren't up to it. She decided, finally, to write him a note. Slip it under his door, where he would find it as soon as he came in, and ask if he would wait for her to come down in the morning.

She struggled over it, using a piece of Pam's drawing paper, sitting at the kitchen table. "Dear Mr. Chellmand . . ." No, she crossed that out. "Dear Sam: I must talk to you. You said you would help me, and I do need help. I will be down by six-thirty in the morning; could you meet me in the kitchen then?" She debated over an ending, finally settling for simply signing her name.

Now to get it under his door without being seen. That Aunt Elsa would disapprove she had no doubt, and Beatrice . . . she shuddered at the thought of how Beatrice might react if she suspected that Cillay was allying herself with someone else against her.

It went without saying that she would go up the back stairs. Pam was already asleep; luckily she slept as well as thought like a child. Cillay climbed in her stocking feet, leaving her shoes on the landing, so that no one would hear her. Aunt Elsa, she knew, was watching television, but the others had all gone to their rooms, she thought. It wouldn't do to have one of them ask brightly at the breakfast table why she had been poking something under Mr. Chellmand's door late at night.

One of the bulbs in the upper hall was burned out, so that it was dimmer than usual. There was a light under Miss Appleton's door, and from Mrs. Sanding's room she could hear music playing softly on the portable radio. None of the rooms had private baths, and they must all come through the hall to reach the bathrooms, so that she ran the risk of being intercepted at any time. Her pulses quickened, Cillay hurried along the corridor, and bent to poke the folded sheet of paper under the door of Sam Chellmand's room. A board creaked under her weight as she stopped there and she hesitated, startled.

"Who's there?"

The voice, Beatrice's, coming out of the darkness of the front stairwell, was sharply interrogative. Cillay stood, glancing frantically toward the doorway onto the stairs at the other end of the hall, and knew she could never reach it in time. Hopelessly, knowing he kept it locked at all times, she never the less tried the knob to Sam's door. She had no excuse for being on this floor at this time of night, no excuse at all.

The knob, as she expected, resisted her efforts. And then, incredibly, a key was turned from the inside and the door swung silently inward (a non-squeaking door in this house?). Before Cillay could do more than utter a small gasp, she had been pulled into the room.

It was dark, and her instinctive reaction was to scream as strong hands held her, but one of them clamped itself over her mouth. After only a few seconds she realized that it was Sam . . . she recognized the scent of his shaving lotion and the tall, hard shape of him. When she collapsed against him he removed his hand from her mouth, patting it gently with a single finger to urge her to silence.

She needed no particular urging. She could hear Beatrice in the hall outside, calling out brusquely, "Who's up here? Cillay? Cillay, is that you?"

Surely no one had seen her. No one would have expected, had they viewed her beginning ascent from the kitchen, that she was going anywhere but up to bed on the third floor. How, then . . . ?"

Sam still held her with an arm around her waist, her shoulders against his chest. Good grief, she thought, better caught in the corridor than in here . . . what would they all make of *this?*

"Mr. Chellmand?" Beatrice rapped on the door. "Mr. Chellmand?"

Sam's hands guided her, silently, across the darkened room. It was not, she saw now, completely dark, for there was some moonlight filtering in through the curtains. He bent to push her toward the floor . . . behind a desk.

Cillay obediently dropped to her knees, wishing they would stop shaking.

"Mr. Chellmand?" Beatrice rattled the doorknob, and the door opened under her hand, for he had not had time to relock it. Beneath the desk Cillay saw the crack of light appear along the edge of the door. "Are you in there?"

Sam spoke as if sleepily. "Yes? Just a minute, let me get a light."

When he turned it on he was sitting on the edge of the bed, rubbing a hand through his tousled hair, yawning.

"Yes, come in, what is it?"

"There's a telephone call for you. Long distance."

"Oh . . . let me get my shoes. I'll be right there." Either Sam actually had been sleeping moments before or he was a consummate actor.

"I thought I heard someone in the hall . . . have you seen Cillay?"

"Cillay? Oh, the little girl. No, I've been asleep. I haven't seen anyone."

She could see his feet, sliding into shoes, the shoes being tied. Then he stood up and walked out of her sight. There was a click, and the light went out.

"I hope it's a person to person call, or they'll be running up a hell of a phone bill . . . what made you think the girl would be running around on the second floor? She sleeps upstairs, doesn't she?"

"Yes, but she's a snoopy one, and I was sure I heard someone . . ."

Their voices moved away from her, down the hallway toward the front stairs. Cillay rose from her uncomfortable crouching position and ran to the doorway, to peer out through the crack. Sam went on downstairs, but Beatrice lingered at the top of them, glancing back this way. And then, to Cillay's horror, she turned and retraced her steps, coming straight back to this room.

Cillay turned, looking for a hiding place. If Beatrice actually entered the room the desk would be of little use as a hiding place, and she knew the closet door creaked . . .

Thank God for high, old fashioned beds. She was on her stomach, rolling under it, without further thought. And then, as she heard Beatrice step on the weak board outside the door, she saw the note.

Heaven only knew why Beatrice hadn't seen it before, or perhaps she had and couldn't do anything about it, with Sam standing over it. Right there on the floor, where Beatrice would see it immediately if she opened the door . . .

130

Cillay stretched out an arm as far as it would go and drew in the note, holding it tightly against her side. The movement was none too soon, for the door swung inward and the light was turned back on.

She could follow Beatrice's progress easily enough. She wore slippers, for her bandaged ankle still precluded wearing regular shoes, and although she limped slightly she was moving rapidly and without real difficulty. She paused to look behind the desk, then opened the closet door and peered it.

"She *must* have gone on upstairs," Beatrice muttered under her breath. "The snoopy little bitch."

Cillay held her breath, expecting that any moment Beatrice would bend down and discover her, and then what could she do or say?

Beatrice did not look under the bed. She retraced her steps to the desk and Cillay heard sounds she could not identify, then Beatrice's whispered curse.

"Might have known he'd leave it locked." She had tried to look into Sam's briefcase, which had been atop the desk. There were more sounds . . . the desk drawers being jerked open, immediately closed. (Sam wouldn't have put anything into the desk drawers that would have given away anything about him.) The woman made a disgruntled noise, then crossed to the door and turned off the light, leaving the door as she had found it, slightly ajar.

Weak with relief, Cillay had to wait a few moments to allow her heart to settle back into its customary place before she could roll out and scramble to her feet.

The coast was clear. She sped down the corridor,

snatched up her waiting shoes, and fled to the safety of her room. Not until she got there did she realize that she still held in her hand the note she had written to Sam Chellmand.

She dropped it onto her dresser and sank onto the bed, tears of despair escaping down her cheeks. She couldn't make another attempt to get it to him tonight. If only she had known he was in his room! How long had he been there? Might she have talked to him at any time during the evening simply by tapping on his door? She could have made some excuse, early in the evening . . . he'd missed dinner, he might want a sandwich, or need towels, or something.

But it was too late now. She'd have to wait until morning.

She had no way of knowing that by morning Sam would be gone.

Beatrice told them all at breakfast.

"He had a long distance call. From Atlanta, Georgia, of all places. Something about his grandfather . . . he's dying, they said, and he had to go right away. He called the airport and got a plane out a little after midnight last night. Said he didn't know when he'd be back."

Cillay was stricken and was terrified that it might show on her face. She kept her eyes on her plate, pushing the bacon and eggs around as if she were eating, but she felt more like being sick.

He had gone to Atlanta, and there was no one, now, to turn to. What if he were gone a long time? Days, or even weeks? She couldn't ask him to find out about Alan, she couldn't depend upon him for any help . . . anything she did would have to be on her own.

She was ashamed to be thinking only of herself and Pam . . . poor Sam, he'd spoken of his grandfather, on one occasion, with affection . . . but she couldn't waste time feeling sorry for him. She was responsible for Pam; she had to get her out of this place before something terrible happened . . . as it would. She knew, with a terrible certainty, that it would. Whatever was going on must eventually culminate in some positive action, some climax. When that happened Cillay didn't want to be here. She wanted to be hundreds of miles away in Serling. The uncertainties of looking for a job and figuring out a way to take care of Pam and work at the same time now seemed infinitely preferable to the uncertainties of what might happen if she stayed here.

She went about her daily chores (Beatrice was once more on crutches this morning, having "strained" the ankle again by walking on it, she said.) thinking up wildly improbable schemes to transport herself and her sister, without funds, back to Illinois.

A bus was out, of course. And she couldn't bring herself at this point (although later she wished to God she had gone out and begged money from strangers in the street) to write to only casual friends and ask to borrow from them.

She considered the likelihood of getting there safely by hitchhiking. Probably they would get rides, all right, once they got outside the city (that was problem enough as it would take every cent she had left for city bus fares to reach the outskirts), for she thought drivers would not be leery of picking up young girls. But young girls, she had been taught, needed to be more than leery of accepting rides with just anyone. Her mother would have been shocked to know she could seriously contemplate such an action. But her mother didn't know what sort of household she had sent her daughter into.

She was very nearly immobilized by fear that evening when she realized that Beatrice was again attempting to get her to drink something she herself had prepared.

She had gotten it into Pam with no difficulty. Cillay found her sister happily drinking the too-sweet cocoa at the kitchen table at bedtime. Her own stomach churned uneasily as she looked at the younger girl, her dark eyes drowsy, her pink cheeks so freshly scrubbed and wholesome looking, smiling at her.

"We poured some for you, too, Cillay," Pam said, nudging a cup toward her. "You can have marshmallows in it. I had *four*."

So much sweetness, enough to cover the taste of anything Beatrice might have put in it. Cillay had no doubt whatever that Beatrice *had* put something in it. She had never fixed anything for them except on the occasions when they had slept so heavily and awakened with thick tongues and dry mouths.

So something was scheduled to happen tonight. What?

Her immediate instinctive reaction was to refuse the drink outright. But quickly on the heels of that reaction came a second one. No. To refuse it would help Beatrice to realize that Cillay suspected the cocoa, to take other steps to put her out of action. Steps unnamed and vague, steps that might be worse than drugged cocoa.

No. Better to pretend to take it, and then to stay awake, to see if this time she could find out what went on when Beatrice prowled the house at night. More searching for the mysterious small object(s)? Or something worse than that?

"Thank you," Cillay said, and accepted the cup. She didn't have to look directly at Beatrice, drinking a cup of her own, to see the satisfaction in the dark hooded eyes.

She pretended to sip at it, letting it barely touch her lips. Pam had already nearly finished hers, and probably there was no harm in her sleeping soundly, anyway. Not that she was likely to get up once she'd fallen asleep in the first place; she never did.

Beatrice was watching her surreptitiously; she would have to take a little of it. She sipped, then had difficulty in forcing herself to swallow it. *Go ahead, she told herself, there can't be much in a single swallow. Don't make her suspicious.*

She faked the next swallow, knowing it was impossible to drink even a little of it, knowing that it was drugged. Pam, quite without conscious intention, gave her the clue as to what to do next.

"I'm hungry, too, Cillay. Couldn't I have a sandwich?"

Cillay rose with alacrity. "Yes, I think I'll make one, too. What do you want, peanut butter and jelly? Or cheese?"

They decided on peanut butter and jelly. Cillay carried her own cup with her to the counter beside the sink and pretended to drink from it while she prepared two sandwiches. And then, with her body shielding the cup from Beatrice's view, she emptied the contents into the sink.

If Beatrice rose from the table she would be able to tell, of course, for Cillay couldn't unobtrusively wash out the sink immediately. Once more she raised her cup, pretending now to drain it and actually having to take the dregs into her mouth; it was a physical impossibility to make herself swallow, and when she choked and spit into the sink she had, at last, an excuse to turn on the water and wash out the cocoa stains.

"Went down the wrong way," she said, and took a drink of water before delivering Pam's sandwich to her.

Beatrice looked quite satisfied. She was not worried that Cillay had missed very much of her special potion. Cillay brought her choking episode to an end and wondered what to do with the sandwich. She'd never felt less like eating in her life.

"I think I'll take mine upstairs and read for a little while. Can't you bring yours along, too, Pam, and eat it on the way? I'm awfully tired tonight."

Pam, as usual, was amenable to any suggestion. They said goodnight to Beatrice and made their way up the back stairs.

Cillay did not, for a time, undress, until it occurred to her that Beatrice might well check to make sure they were both in deep sleep before she began whatever she intended to do. Then she undressed and got into bed, to lie there rigidly, listening to the old house creak and groan, listening for footsteps on the stairs.

136

There were no footsteps. Apparently Beatrice had confidence in her sleeping medication, for she had, after all, watched them drink it.

After a time, when nothing happened, Cillay began to wish she *had* taken some of the cocoa, or that she had a sleeping capsule of her own to take. It was long after one o'clock when she finally began to feel sleepy, and her sleep was broken several times by nightmares she could not remember but which left her shivering and sweating.

Not until broad daylight did she learn that something had, indeed, taken place in the house during the night; but she didn't know whether it had been for this that Beatrice had used her drugs. It was so horrible that she could scarcely credit her senses; if she had been afraid before, it was nothing to what she felt now. For one of the roomers had been brutally murdered and the house had begun to expose its evil heart for all to see.

Chapter 13

Cillay had gone down at the usual time, apprehensively but hopefully, too, for she had seen nor heard nothing during the night to alarm her. A few minutes after she'd started the coffee Mrs. Pomeroy appeared, hair uncombed, incongruously elegant from the neck down in her rose satin dressing gown, looking most disgruntled.

"There's something wrong with the plumbing," she announced angrily. "Which means we'll have to have a plumber out, and you know what *they* cost! I tried to flush the toilet in my bathroom and it flooded all over everything. You'd better go up and tell everyone not to flush anything up there or the whole house will be dripping . . . as soon as it's eight o'clock I'll try to get someone out here to fix it. Go on, it's more important to keep them from flooding the second floor than to have their breakfast on time. No one's going to work from here, anyway, so what does it matter?"

She lifted the lid off the chocolate box sitting on the counter and selected one, biting into it with a juicy sound. "Plumbing in these old places is miserable . . . hard to get at when something goes wrong, too. If the plumber cleans it out and finds that Mrs. Sanding has lost her teeth down the drain, or something equally revolting, I swear I'll present her with the bill! She dropped a washcloth down it once

138

. . . I know she's senile but why should I have to pay plumber's bills because of that?"

Cillay, who did not consider Mrs. Sanding to be in the least senile, said nothing. Her aunt was still grumbling as Cillay headed for the second floor to alert the roomers to the dangers of clogged plumbing.

Alan's room was still vacant, and of course Sam was away, so there were only four people to contact.

Mrs. Sanding appeared promptly, teeth in place, so that wasn't what was causing the difficulty. Cillay explained, and moved on to Miss Appleton's door. There was a scurrying sound, and it was several minutes before the door opened. Mrs. Sanding was right about the wig, for the blue tinted hair was slightly askew. Again Cillay went through her explanation of the problem.

The next door on the far side of the hall was Mrs. Fontana's. Cillay tapped, wondering why everyone hadn't popped out of their rooms, as they must have heard the knocking as it proceeded along the corridor.

There was no answering sound from Mrs. Fontana's room. Cillay rapped again, more firmly, and listening heard nothing at all. Could she be in the bathroom? But no, that door stood ajar, so that wasn't it.

"Mrs. Fontana?" She hesitated, then put a hand on the knob. She hated to walk in on the old lady, but if she were hard of hearing it might be necessary. Aunt Elsa would be furious if a bathroom flooded and the water seeped through the ground floor ceilings.

She pushed gently on the door and it moved inward, revealing the most awful scene Cillay could have imagined.

There had been a struggle. Several of Mrs. Fontana's figurines had been broken, and when the old lady had fallen she had pulled the white spread off the bed, where it had helped to soak up her blood. The front of her night dress was soaked with it, and the stack of pink yarn had been knocked off the table, where it, too, had been dyed red.

There was no question about her being dead. The terrible wound in her chest, and the amount of blood she had lost, could not have been other than fatal.

Cillay felt the strength fade from her body; she clung to the door frame to keep from falling. Her lips moved soundlessly . . . *oh, my God, my God* . . .

How she managed to control her trembling legs, latch the door, and walk down the front stairs Cillay never knew. She was as white as if it were her own blood now staining that upstairs bedroom.

Beatrice was coming through the lower hall on the way to put a letter in the mail box. "Oh, there you are. Never mind about the plumbing, it's working all right now. I just tried it and everything went down. Probably whatever was clogging the drain has washed on through." She stopped, eyes narrowing as she saw Cillay's face. "What's the matter with you? Are you sick?"

Cillay tried twice before her lips and voice would function. "She's dead . . . Mrs. Fontana . . . she's been . . . stabbed, I think. There's blood all over the room."

Beatrice's only reaction was a widening of her hooded eyes. Then she turned and ran swiftly up the stairs, being gone so short a time that Cillay had scarcely blinked her eyes.

The older woman did not seem to see her but hurried toward the back of the house. Cillay heard her urgent voice, "Pet! Come upstairs at once, it's important!"

"Upstairs?" Mrs. Pomeroy's voice rose in disbelief. "Are you out of your mind? Do you know what it will do to my heart if I climb those stairs?"

"Never the less, you've got to do it. And keep still, for Heaven's sake! This isn't something we want to broadcast to the entire house!"

Mrs. Pomeroy came, puffing and buttoning the front of her dress, her incongruously tiny feet encased in satin slippers. "What is it? What's gone wrong now? Did you find out what was stopping up the plumbing?"

"No. Now be still. I don't want to upset the rest of them . . ."

Beatrice led the way, and it was not until the older woman turned back and beckoned that Cillay followed along behind her aunt. She had no wish to further view that bloody room.

She expected that any moment the old ladies or Mr. Gary would erupt into the hall and demand to know what was going on. The sight of Mrs. Pomeroy above stairs would certainly call for an explanation, and Cillay had no desire to be the one to tell them about Mrs. Fontana.

Mrs. Pomeroy panted and hauled herself up by the railing, her breathing becoming so labored that Cillay worried she might, indeed, have the heart attack she was constantly threatening.

When they had at last gained the second floor Beatrice nearly dragged Elsa Pomeroy along, and when Cillay would have waited outside the fatal room it was Beatrice who jerked her impatiently inside.

Mrs. Pomeroy's eyes widened and even rolled back in her head at the shocking sight; she opened her mouth as if to shriek but Beatrice clamped a hand over it. When she spoke her tone was low but commanding.

"Now don't do anything stupid like fainting, for God's sake! We've got to figure out what to do!"

"The police . . ." Cillay said through numbed lips. "We'll have to call the police."

"The police . . . the police . . ." Her aunt was gasping as if deprived of oxygen.

"Be still and listen to me. Use your heads," Beatrice commanded, scarcely louder than a whisper. "Who did it? Have you given any thought to that? Who did it?"

"A burglar . . ." Mrs. Pomeroy rolled her eyes about the room as if seeking to find the culprit in a corner, still clutching his loot.

"Don't be an ass," Beatrice said cuttingly. "We're on the second floor, nothing's been broken into, the screens are intact . . . and the house was locked last night. Every door of it, every ground floor window. Just as it's always locked."

Elsa Pomeroy gaped at her, one pudgy hand pressed to her massive bosom as if to control her heart beat. "Then what . . . ?"

"It was done by someone in this house. Can't you see that? The police will see it soon enough, if you call them. Someone in this house did it!"

"But why . . . ?"

"Why? After the way she's bragged about her jewels and her diamonds? Twelve hundred dollar rings missing . . . Probably someone wanted one of those pretty trinkets, and hoped to steal it but got caught. Had to kill her to shut her up."

Cillay was shaking her head from side to side. "No. There's no one who would . . . would . . ."

Beatrice sent her a contemptuous, fiery glance. "Well, someone obviously did. God, what a mess! We've got to do something before the others realize something's up . . ."

"The police," Cillay began again, but Beatrice stopped her with a rude gesture.

"No, you fools, not the police. You," she said to Cillay, "of all people shouldn't want that, if you've given it any thought whatever."

"I?" Alarm, unreasoning fear, stirred within her. "What do you mean?"

"I mean there's only one person in this house who could have done such a terrible thing . . . such a *crazy* thing." She lifted her eyes to the ceiling. "That girl upstairs. That crazy sister of yours."

They stared at one another in silence. The drumming of blood in her ears drowned out her own sound of protest. Cillay turned to her aunt, holding out a supplicating hand, but Elsa Pomeroy withdrew from her in horror.

"You think . . . ? Oh, my God, that my own niece should be . . . criminally insane! Oh, what will we do? She'll have to be locked up, put away in one of those places where she can't ever again do anything like this . . . !"

143

"No!" Cillay's cry was torn from her throat, strangled, painful. "It's not true! Pam would never hurt anyone. She didn't do this! What a terrible thing to suggest, and you have no reason, no reason at all . . . !"

"Keep your voice down," Beatrice said tautly, "you'll have the rest of them in here and there'll be no keeping it quiet then! The thing to do is make sure, first, that that's what happened."

"How . . . how can we be sure? If the child's insane she won't necessarily tell us about it, will she?" Mrs. Pomeroy cast an almost apologetic glance at Cillay. "I know she isn't responsible, but the rest of us are, you know. She can't be allowed to run loose . . . I remember how she handled those scissors, and Beatrice said she oughtn't to have them . . . Lord, it could have been any one of us! Murdered in our beds!"

Cillay was too horrified to cry. She kept shaking her head, but they were ignoring her.

"If she did do it she might be simple enough not to realize the significance of her actions," Beatrice was saying. "We can ask her; she may admit it. But even if she doesn't, there must be some traces . . ." She gestured around the room. "No one could have done this without getting blood on themselves. Look. If it wasn't the girl, then maybe we'd better call the police, at that. I mean, if it was one of the other roomers there's no reason to protect them, is there? But if it was this girl . . . well, she'd never go to trial for murder or anything like that, would she? Everybody knows she's mentally deficient . . . she can't be held responsible for her actions . . ."

144

"But they'd have to lock her up," Mrs. Pomeroy pointed out. "They couldn't let her run loose any longer. She might kill someone else. I certainly couldn't continue to have her running loose in my rooming house . . . I wouldn't have any roomers! As far as that goes, who's ever going to want to sleep in this room again? Or in my house, if they know a murder was committed here? Oh, dear heaven, what shall we do?"

"No, no, no . . ." Cillay's murmur was a monotone of pain.

"You stay here, Pet," Beatrice said decisively. "We'll go up and question the girl. And if she *did* do it . . . well, we'll have to figure out what to do. Cillay, are you going to come with me to see your sister?"

"I can't stay here alone with . . . that," Mrs. Pomeroy said, but Beatrice cut through her words like flame through tissue paper.

"You'll have to. There's no time to waste, we've got to decide what to do and do it quickly."

She gave Mrs. Pomeroy no second chance to talk her way out of waiting there with poor Mrs. Fontana's mutilated body. Cillay cast an agonized glance of appeal toward her aunt, but Mrs. Pomeroy was concerned with herself and her rooming house; she did not even see Cillay's face.

They found Pam asleep. Cillay moved to waken her, but Beatrice was ahead of her, bending over the bed, shaking the young girl's shoulder. "Pam! Wake up!"

There was no way, Cillay had to admit, that Beatrice could have planted any evidence at the time.

145

And evidence there was, for when Pam sat up on the edge of the bed, her bare feet searching for slippers, both of them could see the spattering of blood on the lower part of Pam's nightgown. There was even some on the bottoms of her feet. Cillay stared at her sister in a sick horror, unable to speak, for there in plain sight on the dresser was a large pair of scissors with an unmistakable stain on the sharp blades.

"Pam, do you know what's happened to Mrs. Fontana?" Beatrice asked. For once her voice, when speaking to the girl, was not brusque but quite ordinary.

"Mrs. Fontana?" Pam yawned up at them, puzzled.

"Yes. You remember, the lady who knits pink things. You know the one I mean?"

"Yes. I remember her."

"What's happened to her?" Beatrice pressed. "Did you know she was hurt?"

She will deny any knowledge of it, Cillay thought, *and Beatrice will manufacture evidence of it somehow . . . she must have brought the scissors here earlier, and Pam's nightgown . . . she's trying to make it look as if Pam has done something she would never have done . . .*

"Mrs. Fontana is hurt," Beatrice repeated, and an unexpected expression came into Pam's face.

Bewilderment, as if she were trying to think how she knew. "Yes. She had . . . blood all over her. A lot of blood."

Cillay swayed, reaching out a hand to the bed post for support. How could Pam possibly know that?

"Tell us what she looked like," Beatrice suggested,

146

her eyes searching out Cillay as if to say, *see, what did I tell you?*

"She . . . she was lying on the floor, and there was blood all over her," Pam said obediently, frowning. "And all that pink wool she uses to make sweaters was all over the floor, too."

"You must have stepped in some of the blood," Beatrice said, indicating her feet.

Pam lifted a foot to look at it. "Yes. I guess I'd better wash it off, hadn't I, Cillay?"

Cillay could not, to save her life, have replied.

"Yes," Beatrice said for her. "Go wash your feet, and then get dressed. Cillay, get down stairs and feed the old women . . . cereal, anything. Then we'll have to get together and decide what we're going to do with . . . it."

It, of course, referred to Mrs. Fontana's body. And there would also have to be a decision as to what to do about Pam.

"Go on," Beatrice said more sharply. "It won't do to have them suspect there's anything wrong. We'll tell them Mrs. Fontana isn't feeling well this morning, until we can think of something better . . . but they'll have to be fed. Feed her . . ." jerking her head in Pam's direction, ". . . in the kitchen, so she won't talk to them."

Cillay shook her head. "I can't." Her voice was no more than a croak. "I can't feed anyone. Please . . ."

Beatrice straightened with an exasperated sigh. "All right, then I'll have to do it. But get her cleaned up and bring her down to eat in the kitchen, and as soon as the old ladies are settled in the dining room we'll have to have a conference. Hurry it up, now."

147

With a conspiratorial glance at Cillay, she wrapped a handkerchief around the scissors and concealed them as best she could in her deep apron pocket.

For several minutes after Beatrice had gone neither of them said anything. Pam stood up and stripped off her nightgown, dropping it over the end of the bed.

"Run the water for me, Cillay? Until it gets warm. I don't want to wash my feet in cold water."

As if mechanically controlled, Cillay moved into the adjoining bathroom and turned on the tap, then came back to the bedroom where her sister was getting dressed.

"Pam . . ." She cleared her throat and tried again before she spoke loudly enough to be heard over the sound of the running water. "Pam . . . how do you know about Mrs. Fontana? Were you there?"

"Was I where? Do my buttons, please?"

Cillay's fingers fumbled with the back of her sister's blouse. "Were you in Mrs. Fontana's room, Pam? Is that where you saw her?"

"In her room, yes. On the floor. I don't know why she was on the floor."

"Did you . . . touch her?"

"Oh, no. I didn't want to touch her." Pam twisted to look into Cillay's face. "She was all bloody."

"How did she get that way, Pam?" There was some explanation, there had to be! Cillay thought desperately. "You didn't hurt her, did you?"

"No, of course not. I never hurt anyone, Cillay. She was bleeding all over her nightdress and her wool."

"But you didn't hurt her? You didn't . . ." she took a deep breath and forced herself to phrase the question. "You didn't take those scissors to her room, did you, Pam?"

"No." She screwed up her face thoughtfully, fastening her skirt. "It was funny. I don't know how I got there at all. But I remember seeing her there, on the floor."

"How did the scissors get here, on your dresser?"

Pam considered carefully. "I don't remember any scissors. I wasn't cutting anything, was I?"

Pam had been drugged last night, Cillay remembered now, as some of the shock began to fade and her hope to return. Had Beatrice somehow taken her there, in a groggy state, and showed her the scene of such carnage, then brought her back to bed after deliberately leading her through the mess so that her gown and feet would be contaminated?

For one thing she knew about Pam. Pam never lied. She was, quite simply, incapable of it, for lying requires imagination, and Pam had none. She had always, for her entire life, told the literal truth as she saw it about everything. And if she said she hadn't harmed Mrs. Fontana, she was telling the truth.

Beatrice was responsible for that terrible crime. Cillay knew it as surely as she knew her sister was innocent. But how many people would be convinced of that? How many people would take her word and the word of a mentally retarded girl against the word of Beatrice?

She helped Pam wash her feet, by this time feeling almost nothing at the thought of getting any of Mrs. Fontana's blood on her own hands. It was too late to be squeamish. She had been a fool not to have gotten out of this house the moment she realized there was something strange going on. How could she have allowed Beatrice to drug her drinks and set up something like this? She had no idea why anyone should have wanted to do such a thing, unless it was to take Mrs. Fontana's jewelry, but she wouldn't get away with it. No, indeed she would not, Cillay resolved, and her teeth came together grimly and she rolled up her sister's nightgown and stripped the sheets off the bed in case they also carried some telltale trace of the blood, and stood wondering what to do with them. For she was determined that whatever happened they would not be preserved as evidence against Pam.

Chapter 14

She was not, however, quick enough. Beatrice met her on the stairs, smiling rather grimly.

"Yes, we'll have to hide those," she said, and took the bloodstained garment and sheets out of Cillay's hands. "It might be possible to burn them . . . we'll have to see. I'll think of something."

Hating her, fearing her, Cillay could not say "I'll bet you will," nor could she retain them against Beatrice's wishes. Why hadn't she moved more quickly?

"They're all very curious," Beatrice went on, as one conspirator to another, as they descended to the kitchen. "I told them Mrs. Fontana wasn't feeling well, and that you'd overslept and then burned yourself so I was making do. I've left some cereal on the table for your sister; do you want some before we talk?"

Cillay shook her head. The last thing in the world she wanted was food; she was sure it would never stay down.

"All right, then. Come along to your aunt's room while your sister eats. She should be all right long enough for us to do that, don't you think? But we're going to have to watch her very closely from now on."

Pam seemed not to realize that anything was wrong. She took her place at the table and began sugaring her corn flakes unconcernedly. Beatrice had already gone on to Mrs. Pomeroy's room, but Cillay lingered.

"Don't you remember anything about how you got to Mrs. Fontana's room, Pam? Did someone take you there?"

"I don't know. It was like a dream, sort of . . . I wasn't all the way awake, but not sleeping, either. I remember my feet were cold."

"Was Beatrice there? In Mrs. Fontana's room?" Cillay asked urgently. "Do you remember seeing Beatrice?"

Pam's face clouded with the effort of trying to remember. "I don't like Beatrice."

"No, dear, I know that. But was she there, when Mrs. Fontana was . . . lying on the floor?"

Pam licked sugar off her spoon. "I don't think so. I don't remember her."

"Aunt Elsa, then? Was Aunt Elsa there?"

Pam shook her head. "No. Why was I there, Cillay?"

She wished to God she knew the answer to that. Or, perhaps, in a way, she did, Cillay thought, leaving her sister to eat in peace. Beatrice had set it up, the entire thing. She had almost certainly killed Mrs. Fontana herself and disposed of her own bloody garments. (She'd been truthful about that part of it; no one could have accomplished such a brutal murder without getting blood on herself.) She had then taken poor drugged Pam to the room so that she would remember it, would be able to describe it. To convince me, Cillay reasoned disjointedly, to make me believe Pam had done it. But why does she want me to think my sister is a murderer? And how had

152

she gotten Pam there without Pam realizing she was there, too?

She had to think, before they got her into that room and tried to force the rest of their foul plans down her throat, what she was going to do. Her instinct was to fight: for Pam's freedom, for her own. But caution held her back.

They'd had time to plan this. Beatrice and Aunt Elsa. She could no longer doubt that Elsa Pomeroy was in on it, too. Beatrice couldn't have managed everything on her own. They had to have worked it out together, something they wanted to do with Pam and Cillay. To fight them, openly, would probably be futile, when they held all the cards and she knew so little.

No, better to pretend (did she have to pretend?) to be in a state of shock and horror; listen to what they proposed, do whatever necessary to protect Pam for the moment. And then, when they might complacently take her cooperation for granted, find some way to break free of them.

Sam would be back in a few days; whatever mysterious reasons of his own he had for being in this house, she was sure he was not involved in a murder. And Sam, she remembered with a flicker of hope, was a lawyer. He would know what to do to keep them from taking Pam away, from branding her a murderess. He, at least, would not swallow Beatrice's preposterous stories.

It wasn't easy to sit in that too warm, heavily scented, cluttered room and listen to them. Mrs. Pomeroy sat on the green velvet settee (it had been intended for two people, but she occupied almost all of the space herself), while Cillay perched on the edge of the boudoir chair with the peacock blue seat. Even at a time like this, Elsa Pomeroy could not refrain from eating chocolates, one after another, sucking out their soft insides with disgusting noises, then daintily licking her fingers.

"Well," Beatrice said, pausing in her pacing about the room, "there are, so far as I can see, two things we can do. We can, first of all, call the police and tell them one of our roomers has been murdered. We wouldn't have to tell them who did it; they'd find that out quickly enough for themselves."

Particularly, Cillay said silently, *when they find the bloodstained nightgown in whatever secure place dear Beatrice has hidden it, and those horrible scissors . . .*

"Or," Beatrice went on with the air of one who is genuinely trying to find the best solution, "we can try to cover it up. Keep anyone from knowing what's happened. You realize that's the only way we'll keep your sister out of a mental hospital?"

She didn't have to pretend to be unable to reply to that. *Oh, Mama, it was too much to ask of me! I don't know how to do it, to keep Pam safe!*

"But how? How can we possibly keep the police from learning about it?" Mrs. Pomeroy was asking. As if they hadn't rehearsed the entire thing ahead of time, Cillay mused bitterly.

"By not telling them, of course. Oh, I know there's more to it than that. But there's more to consider than just the girl, Pet. The reputation of your house . . . we barely make ends meet as it is. Can you imagine how long the others would stay, if they knew what had happened? Or how many new roomers we'd get, if the word got out?"

Mrs. Pomeroy shuddered dramatically. "It would be a disaster . . . a total disaster."

She was overdoing it; she was being too dramatic. The more either of them said, the more thoroughly Cillay was convinced that they had plotted this between them, that they had set a trap for her and she had fallen into it. Blindly, stupidly, but totally. Dear God, was there any way out of it?

"Yes," Beatrice was agreeing, "in more ways than one. But consider this. We can tell the others that Mrs. Fontana has gone away . . . make it a hospital trip in the middle of the night, when they're all asleep . . . and then we'll report that she's died almost right away. So they won't want to go and visit her, you see."

"They'd expect to go to the funeral, in that case," Cillay put in, and could have bitten her tongue for her foolishness. She wasn't supposed to be thinking, or reasoning, or throwing obstacles in their way. *Just listen,* she told herself, *listen and don't say anything.*

Beatrice frowned. "Yes. You're right. We'd have to think of something . . . like shipping her body out of state to be buried, or something."

"She hasn't any relatives to request that; everyone knows she's all alone," Mrs. Pomeroy stated. It was almost as if they'd written out a script, they picked up cues from one another so readily. Cillay wondered if they had.

"Yes. Which is all to our advantage, in that no one will come around inquiring after her," Beatrice added. "We can say she made provisions in her will to be buried with her husband . . . where's he buried?"

"I don't know, but there must be something in her belongings that will give us a clue. But that still leaves the biggest problem of all: what are we to do with her body? If we don't turn it over to the police? We can't leave it where it is, not for any time at all."

"No. We'll have to think about that. But those are our choices: the police, and sending the girl to an institution for life, or covering it up. I mean, it isn't as if we're letting a murderer go free, exactly; we know who did it, and we won't turn her loose on society."

As if Beatrice cared a fig for society. Cillay was breathing rapidly, shallowly, trying to force her brain to work. Unfortunately, it was still in more of a state of shock than she had hoped it would be at this point. Useless, absolutely useless, to try to plan while Beatrice was walking up and down, talking to her, pointing out what would happen to Pam if Cillay didn't go along with their ideas.

For it was true: Pam could easily be locked up for this terrible crime. The idea sent Cillay into panic, and it took all of her self-control to put it down.

"We have to make up our minds right now," Beatrice was going on inexorably. "I've turned off the heat to her room but even so the body will begin to deteriorate very rapidly. We've got to get it out of there, if we're going to. And every minute it's there we run the danger of someone trying to go in and talk to her, see how she is. I told them she'd asked not to be disturbed, but that won't hold that dreadful Mrs. Sanding off for long, I'm afraid."

That dreadful Mrs. Sanding. Dear little Mrs. Sanding, who was a positive saint compared to Beatrice.

For a moment Cillay toyed with the idea of asking Mrs. Sanding for help, but immediately discarded the notion. What could a frail little old lady do? And she, too, might be won over by Beatrice's persuasive testimony and a glimpse of the evidence, in spite of her dislike of Beatrice herself.

"She's your sister," Mrs. Pomeroy said. "What do you think? You must have a voice in this, as she's your responsibility."

"I don't know," Cillay said dully. "How can we hope to cover it up? How can we possibly do it, just make her disappear, with no one asking any questions?"

"She's an old lady. She has no friends, no relatives. She will simply go to the hospital and die. Why should anyone question it? Especially if we all stick together."

Cillay's mouth was dry. "And what about Pam? What will happen to her?"

"Why, nothing," Beatrice said blandly. "We'll have to have her under constant observation, of course, one or the other of us. To make sure she doesn't get hold of a scissors again, or a knife."

"She'd ought to be kept away from the roomers," Mrs. Pomeroy contributed. "To be sure she doesn't talk about it, you know. She did talk about it to you, she might to someone else."

Why did they think Cillay would believe they were so solicitous about her sister? Neither of them liked her, neither of them had been happy to have the two girls in the house, in spite of the amount of work they had piled on Cillay's shoulders. What in the name of God were they up to? For this murder had taken place during last night and was only the latest development; something had been afoot before the girls ever came.

Cillay leaned forward, dropping her face into her hands. She did not trust herself to keep the hatred out of her face, she must not let them see how she felt about them . . .

"We'll take a vote," Beatrice said. "That's the only fair way to do it. We'll take a vote."

As if it really mattered to them, one way or the other, if Pam were to be shut up for the rest of her life. It was less than nothing to Beatrice if the police took her away; Cillay doubted that it would have any tremendous long-range effect on the future of the rooming house if it were known that a murder had taken place here. And the police just might be able to determine what had actually happened here . . .

"I vote to dispose of the body and cover up the whole story," Beatrice said firmly. "It will be better for us all if no one ever knows about it."

Unexpectedly, Elsa Pomeroy's voice wavered. "But it's taking such a chance . . . we'd be safer, you and I, Beatrice, if we turned her over to the police. I mean, after all, *we* had nothing to do with her death . . . but we'll be . . . accomplices or something, won't we, if we don't report it?"

She didn't fool Cillay for a moment. They'd planned this, too, expecting that if she herself had any doubts about the wisdom of covering up such a crime her aunt's hesitation would swing Cillay over to Beatrice's side.

"Yes. We'd all three be equally guilty," Beatrice

158

admitted. "But we wouldn't plan to get caught, would we? We wouldn't have to go through all that dreadful publicity, and police through the house, and watching them take the child away to a mental hospital . . ."

This would have been far more convincing had Beatrice at any time showed any civility, let alone friendliness, toward Pam. Cillay suspected that Beatrice was enjoying her acting job, but dared not look full into her eyes to verify this, afraid of what her own eyes would reveal.

She raised her head, looking at the space between the two women.

"Do whatever you like," she said dejectedly.

"You have to vote," the younger of the two women said. "It's got to be partly your decision, too, so you can't say we forced you into anything."

That might have had its humorous aspects if it hadn't been so ghastly. She dared not look at either of them but dropped her eyes and kept her voice low.

"All right. I don't want her locked up. What do you want me to do? About . . . concealing the body?"

"You'll have to help get her downstairs, probably," Beatrice said, unable to conceal her satisfaction at Cillay's capitulation. "But not until tonight . . . not unless we can think of some way to get them all out of the house for a while."

"Good grief, they've never all left the house at once," Elsa Pomeroy protested.

"Well, try to think of something that would lure them all away. Anyway, Cillay, you'd better get back to the kitchen, and remember, if you meet anyone, you didn't show up at breakfast because you burned yourself. I'll let you know when I've worked out a plan of some sort."

"Where . . . where are you going to put the . . . body?"

"I don't know yet," Beatrice replied, but Cillay could tell by her tone that she was lying. She already knew what she was going to do. They were handling all this so smoothly . . . so *expertly* . . . that she had the sudden shocking idea that they might have done it all before. Which was absurd, of course. Wasn't it?

"All right. Let me know, when . . ."

She didn't finish it. She didn't have to. She'd have given a lot to have listened in on their conversation after she'd left the room, but that was impossible for they left the door open. Cillay walked away without looking back, while her mind raced in an effort to figure out the best thing to do.

Common sense told her that the best thing, the right thing, the *lawful* thing to do was to report Mrs. Fontana's death to the authorities. Let the police, who were equipped to do it, investigate the murder and determine the guilty party. If Pam were innocent, as she was, no one could prove otherwise.

Not even, the cold thread of fear running through her reminded, if Beatrice has manufactured evidence? Like the bloody scissors and the blood on Pam's nightclothes, which would certainly prove to be the same type as Mrs. Fontana's?

Cillay was trying to be logical but she was, in actuality, nearly insane with fear. She knew that her aunt and Beatrice had deliberately played upon her

160

apprehensions about her sister's future, exploiting her dread of having the younger girl committed to an asylum. But she was completely in the dark as to Beatrice's *purpose* in all this . . . she had something to gain, no doubt, from Mrs. Fontana's death, especially if there was no family to claim her possessions . . . but why had they allowed the girls to come here in the first place and what did they hope for now by threatening Pam?

They intend to force me to do something, she thought. But what? *What?*

Chapter 15

She scarcely knew how she got through the day. The old people apparently had accepted the story of Mrs. Fontana's indisposition, and no one bothered Cillay so long as she stayed in the kitchen.

She heard Mrs. Sanding once, requesting that anyone who saw the mailman let her know, as her Social Security check was due and she wanted to cash it as soon as it came.

The mailman. She had, Cillay knew, no way of getting in touch with Sam by telephone. Even if he were here in town, readily available, Beatrice would hear her trying to call. But could she get a message in the mail to him? Surely his office knew where he was, or would be the first place he would contact upon his return.

Oh, Sam, Sam, she whimpered, giving way for a few minutes to her longing for him. If only he were here he would know what to do . . .

But he was not here, and by evening Beatrice would have figured out a way to dispose of that body upstairs and Cillay herself would be an accomplice to the crime.

Pam, not to be allowed out of her sight, was sketching pictures at the kitchen table. Cillay asked for one of her sheets of paper and sat down for a moment to compose a brief note. Her pencil moved rapidly over the paper, for she knew that at any time Beatrice might pop in to check on her.

"Dear Sam: Mrs. Fontana is dead and they are pretending to think that Pam did it. You were right. We should not have come to this house, but now I don't know how to get us away. Please help me." She signed it, simply, "Cillay."

There was a packet of envelopes, the stamped kind bought from the post office, on the back of the counter, and as she reached for them she knocked against the box of chocolates in front of them. The box slid over the edge of the counter before she could stop it, spilling its contents onto the floor.

Hastily Cillay began to pick up the chocolates and put them back, and then she saw that more than candies had been in the box. Under the top layer of sweets there were three small passbooks . . . savings account passbooks.

Terrified as she was of being intercepted before she could mail the note to Sam, Cillay could not resist checking them quickly. She had seen them all before. The first was the red covered book Aunt Elsa had had: she flipped it open and saw the name inside, Elsa S. Pomeroy, and the balance, four thousand, one hundred and twenty-two dollars. The second was the one she had found in the telephone book, the one which had once held fourteen thousand dollars but which had been closed. And the third was the one she had seen on Mrs. Fontana's dresser, the one showing a balance of sixty-two thousand dollars. Now she saw, with a startled glance, that only yesterday Mrs. Fontana had withdrawn ten thousand dollars.

How had they induced her to do that? An investment, perhaps, or something to do with repairing or resetting her jewelry? Cillay would have been willing to wager anything she had that the money withdrawn from Mrs. Fontana's account was now in Beatrice's possession. *And Aunt Elsa's.*

She dumped the bank books and the chocolates into their container, quickly scribbled Sam's name and office address on an envelope, and hid it in her apron pocket for the walk to the front door.

She almost made it. The mailman was coming up the walk, and if she could have met him and put the envelope into his hand . . .

But Beatrice came out of the front parlor, her eyes probing, not seeing the envelope but alert for any action on Cillay's part . . . there was no chance to pass it over without being seen. And the one thing she could not do at the moment was to increase Beatrice's suspicions. A woman who could coldbloodedly murder a helpless old lady . . . and deliberately blame it on an equally helpless retarded girl . . . would do anything to accomplish what she sought to do.

Cillay hesitated, wondering how she could possibly get the envelope into the mail . . . perhaps when Beatrice had taken the incoming letters she would immediately leave, as she usually did . . . and Cillay could follow the mailman down the steps . . .

But Beatrice, of course, did not leave. There were several letters, and she flipped through them without interest, her body blocking the open doorway. There was nothing for Cillay to do but retreat to the kitchen, the message unmailed.

She had blundered into something so dark and devious here that she was afraid to learn what it was. What, to have led to the death of poor Mrs. Fontana? Theft of her jewelry, which she had foolishly boasted of, and the money she had removed from the bank? But there had been other things before that . . . the mysterious searchings which had literally ripped apart every room on the third floor, the drugged drinks (Had Beatrice drugged everyone in the house last night? Surely the roomers on the same floor must have heard a struggle which had resulted in an old woman's death.), Sam's peculiar actions . . . what did they all add up to? For one thing, that Beatrice had planned Mrs. Fontana's death very carefully. So carefully that Cillay could not help wondering if it were the first time she had planned a death . . . and wondering, too, if it would be the last.

She had been a fool not to trust Sam, not to have insisted that he tell her why he had tried to warn her away from this house, not to have told him that she knew he had been the one who locked her out of Aunt Elsa's room (wouldn't that have given her leverage to find out what he was doing?) . . . *what did it all add up to?*

She had been a fool to have come here at all; she was, after all, nineteen years old and strong and healthy. Granted that she wasn't trained to do anything in particular in the way of earning a living; Monica wasn't, either, and she'd gotten a job that paid enough for her to have an apartment and a car . . .

She hadn't been thinking clearly, either before or after her mother died. It is a dreadful thing to have to continue to live with someone you love, knowing she is dying and there is nothing you can do, either to prevent her death or to eliminate her suffering. But it was no excuse for not having begun to plan . . . all those months ago, when she first knew that she would soon be totally responsible for Pam. She ought to have found a job then. She ought to have swallowed her pride and gone to friends for help . . . for a loan, for assistance in finding employment, for help with Pam. Instead of which she had let her mother write to Aunt Elsa, she had used up part of her pitiful supply of cash to come all this way, looking for a family she had not found in this strange aunt, looking for a home and security that had not materialized.

But she had done none of these things. She was here, now, and she had to find some way out of this mess.

She thought, off and on, about giving up and calling the police. If they came now, before the body was moved, there must be some clue that would lead them to the true murderer. They might take Pam away, temporarily, but they would surely not be able to do anything to her, for any psychiatric examination would reveal her gentle nature, her total inability to participate in anything violent or forceful.

Once Cillay moved through the hallway toward the phone, having made up her mind to call the authorities, but Beatrice was there. Smiling in false cordiality, asking if Cillay were looking for her.

She's making sure I don't do anything foolish, Cillay thought. *And once I've "helped," or even knowingly stood by while they dispose of poor Mrs. Fontana, I will be as guilty as they. And what will they do then?*

166

It was incredible that none of the others realized anything was wrong. Miss Appleton was primarily engaged in her flirtation with Mr. Gary, and he seemed to be basking under her attentions. While Mrs. Sanding dealt out innumerable hands of solitaire . . . red queen on a black king, black four on a red five . . . until Cillay wanted to scream at them, "There's a dead woman upstairs, and Beatrice killed her! How can you all sit here as if nothing has happened?"

Perhaps Beatrice suspected how she felt, for she was never far away. There was never a moment when Cillay might have spoken to one of the others without being overheard.

Aunt Elsa followed her usual routine . . . chocolates and soap operas on the color TV . . . the bovine movements of her fat jowls proof enough to Cillay that the terrible thing upstairs was not as much of a shock to her as she had pretended. She had puffed and panted her way upstairs this morning, to be sure, but she had made it; had she been there when Beatrice had used those dreadful scissors?

And where was Alan? Even now, worried as she was about herself and her sister, Cillay found time to think about Alan, too. He, like Sam, had been here for a purpose, a very specific purpose . . . they were searching for something, and Sam had considered it sufficiently dangerous to want Alan out of it. What if Sam were wrong and Alan had never gotten out of it? What if he had come home from school early, as he had planned, and determined to make one last try to find whatever it was he was looking for? What if he had been intercepted by Beatrice or Aunt Elsa, who had been here all day? What would they have done if they had discovered that the boy had stumbled onto their secrets?

Cillay could not believe that either Sam or Alan, in their searching, would have destroyed and demolished, as the searcher of the third floor had done. That was, she felt sure, Beatrice's work. It had the look of the woman's rage, her impotent fury at not being able to locate whatever it was she sought.

Sam had searched the kitchen, and left it so slightly out of order that no one would have noticed, except that Cillay had so recently arranged things herself in a more precise manner than was usual in this house.

Did they search for the same thing? She thought of the bank book she had found, the one which indicated that all funds had been withdrawn from the account, and Beatrice's brief, uncontrolled outburst . . . "It can't have been closed! There should be at least . . . !"

The money that she had expected to be in the bank account. Was that what Beatrice looked for? But the money had been in Elsa Pomeroy's account, and she must know what had become of her own money . . .

While Cillay tried to force her brain to think, to reason, it had stubbornly refused. And now, while her thoughts wandered aimlessly, that light bulb of the comic strips had suddenly turned on inside her head. Why hadn't it occurred to her before? For it fit, it explained so many things . . .

She felt hot and cold all at once and trembled with

the blinding certainty growing stronger by the moment.

Elsa Pomeroy, "Pet," was not her aunt at all. Elsa Pomeroy, who appeared in dreams as a gigantic black widow spider, was an imposter.

And if this were so, Cillay thought with a horror that threatened her supply of oxygen, where was her real aunt? What had they done with her, "Pet" and Beatrice?

Chapter 16

The real Elsa Pomeroy had been expecting them. Whether or not the telegram had gone astray, she had known from Dorothy Montand's letter some three months previously that the girls would be coming to her soon. There would have been no reason for her to be surprised when they showed up, and she would most assuredly have spoken to any assistant about their coming, preparing rooms for them.

Cillay sat on her kitchen stool, not seeing Pam bent over the paper she was coloring, forgetting the pan of potatoes she was peeling. She hadn't lost the letter, then; Beatrice had made sure she would be asleep by dosing her milk, and had slipped into the room during the night and stolen it. For they would want to know what Elsa Pomeroy had written. A friendly, welcoming letter, assuring them that she had plenty of room and would be glad to have them, a letter stating that she had recently revised her will and would leave what she possessed to Cillay, to enable her to take care of her sister when the time should come that Elsa herself could not make a home for them. A letter that had mentioned her brother in terms that left no doubt the missive was written by Elsa herself.

Yes, they'd had to have that letter in order to know what Elsa was supposed to have said. And they had searched through the desk in the cluttered room until they found the letter Dorothy had written to Elsa.

Her thoughts were flying like autumn leaves in a high wind, dipping, swirling, lighting on first one thing and then another. The paper she had found in the back yard the day Beatrice had injured her ankle. Not Beatrice, but "Pet" practicing the signature she hoped would enable her to withdraw the money from the bank accounts . . . no wonder Beatrice raged when she discovered it was already gone.

Where was it? Here in this house, hidden away somewhere? Why had her aunt withdrawn it, and what had she done with it? *Had she been killed for it?* Had they disposed of the real Elsa Pomeroy the way they intended to dispose of poor Mrs. Fontana?

A shudder ran through Cillay's slim body, and she was not aware of it. She was remembering the conversation she had overheard . . . *"We've got to do something about her, Pet! Maybe you're willing to take a chance, but I'm not! You can't be so stupid you don't see how dangerous it can be!"*

Had they intended to kill her by a fall down the stairs? What other delightful surprises did Beatrice have in store for her? Police to be called in? Not a chance of it, "Pet" had only suggested it to frighten her into believing that to do so would be to sentence Pam to a life in a mental institution. "Pet" could not afford any sort of police investigation!

Had they taken Cillay's money to prevent her leaving? But Beatrice did not want her here, she was dangerous . . . But of course. If she left, they would have no control over her actions or her tongue

. . . what had she seen that she might mention elsewhere, something that would be dangerous to "Pet" and Beatrice?

The butcher had said that Mrs. Pomeroy had closed her boarding house, gave the roomers only days to find new places to live. How had they managed that? Had Beatrice been, in fact, assistant to her aunt? Had she been the one to give the roomers their notice to move? And had she then, after somehow installing "Pet" as Elsa Pomeroy, re-opened the place with all new roomers, people who couldn't have told whether she was the real Mrs. Pomeroy or an imposter?

If so, with what object in mind?

That, at least, seemed clear enough. Mrs. Pomeroy had had money . . . quite a good deal of money. Part of it was in the bank, and they'd practiced forging her name, hoping that when presented along with the passbook it would be accepted . . . she was, after all, a sick old woman with an unsteady hand.

And after Elsa Pomeroy was gone, her bank account milked dry, there might be others like poor Mrs. Fontana . . . people with some money, some valuable possessions . . . who had no relatives, no close friends, no one to check on them . . .

They had somehow induced Mrs. Fontana to withdraw a substantial sum from the bank. But she had not willingly handed it over to them . . . had they talked her into something which, on further consideration, she had decided was ill advised? And had Beatrice then, with her almost ungovernable temper, stabbed her to death and taken the money?

172

Had she intended to frame Pam for this from the start, from the moment she doctored the cocoa to keep them from overhearing or interfering? Or had the murder been a spur of the moment thing, and the following events a masterful improvisation?

She was sick, sick all the way through, but her brain had come out of its stupor, it was functioning again. She drew a long breath, sure that a major part of her suppositions had some foundation in fact. And knowing that "Pet" was not her aunt, that she owed her nothing (owed, in fact, her aunt the duty of determining what had become of her) Cillay felt a sense of freedom. She was not hampered by loyalty to anyone. If Sam would only come back, she would tell him everything she knew and everything she suspected. If he were here to discover the truth about these women, she would help him find it.

If only she could get out to mail the letter to him! But perhaps he would be back tomorrow . . . He was flying, and Atlanta was not so far away by plane . . .

She tried not to think that if his grandfather died he might remain in Atlanta for days until the funeral could take place . . . or if the old man lingered on in critical condition Sam might stay by his side . . . It didn't bear thinking of, that Sam might not return in time to help her.

In time . . . she had no way of knowing what the time limit was. But Cillay was sure that Beatrice had plans for her . . . unpleasant plans. If she could simply walk away from this house, take Pam by the hand and head for the nearest police station . . .

But every time she approached a door, or even an open window, one of them was there. Beatrice or "Pet."

It wasn't until late in the afternoon, when she needed to use the kitchen table, that she asked Pam to clear away her drawing things. And she stopped, the blood draining from her face; Pam had drawn a horribly realistic picture, and its primary colors, aside from black and white, were the pink skeins of yarn and the red of blood.

Pam, for all that she had only the mental abilities of a small child, was remarkably talented with a pen or pencil. Not a great artist, of course, but her sketches were clever portrayals of what she saw.

And what Pam had seen was a murder. Perhaps not at the moment it actually took place, but shortly thereafter.

The room was Mrs. Fontana's . . . Cillay recognized the single bed post Pam had drawn. There was the bedspread, pulled from its usual place by Mrs. Fontana's outstretched, clutching fingers . . .

And Mrs. Fontana herself. Even the features were recognizable, for all that they were simply sketched with pencil. Mouth opened in what must have been a scream (Beatrice had to have drugged them all, in preparation for whatever she had intended doing with Mrs. Fontana) and her chest a mass of reddened nightclothes.

But what held Cillay transfixed was not the body of Mrs. Fontana, for she knew Pam had seen that. The interesting thing was that Pam had sketched in another figure . . . a woman's figure, in some

174

sort of long dressing gown. The woman stood to one side, looking down on the body, and in her hand she held a pair of scissors.

"Pam . . ." Her voice was husky and so low that until she repeated her sister's name Pam did not respond. "Pammy . . . why haven't you given her . . . this woman . . . any face?"

"She didn't have a face," Pam replied, and reached again for the red felt pen to touch the blades of the scissors.

She didn't have a face. Cillay's mind raced, considering. Of course, if Beatrice had taken Pam there, in order to let her see the scene, in order to be able to talk about having been there, she would not also want her to remember that Beatrice had been there, too.

"Do you mean," Cillay asked carefully, "that she wore a mask?"

Pam looked at her blankly.

"You know, those things kids wear on their faces at Halloween?"

But Halloween, almost a year ago, was beyond Pam's memory. What would she have used? A stocking over her face? What difference did it make. It had been Beatrice, she was convinced of that. If the over-padded "Pet" had been able to make it upstairs and engage in such a struggle, Pam would never have depicted her as tall and thin. It had to be Beatrice.

"This woman . . . the woman who had no face . . . did she . . . hurt Mrs. Fontana, with the scissors?"

175

Pam considered this seriously, as she did everything. "Would it hurt, to pull the scissors out?"

Cillay's chest ached, and she cast a furtive glance toward the door, for Beatrice and "Pet" had been making it a point, today, of looking in on them frequently.

"Is that what she did? Pulled the scissors out of Mrs. Fontana's chest?"

"Yes."

"Did you touch them? Did you touch the scissors?"

"No."

"Are you sure?"

Puzzled, Pam allowed herself to be distracted from her drawing. She was not used to being pressed to be truthful, for she was never anything else.

"You didn't touch the scissors yourself. Only the woman who had no face touched them."

This was clear enough, and Pam's lips curved in an agreeable smile. "Yes."

"Do you know what she did with them?"

"I don't know. I'm getting hungry, Cillay. May I have an apple?"

Cillay gave it to her, then asked if she might have the drawing to keep.

"Do you like it?" Pam asked, pleased.

Cillay swallowed and forced herself to speak normally. "Yes, I do. Thank you, I'll keep it."

It wouldn't do to have Beatrice see it, she thought. Not with herself sketched in, faceless. And some day, when Beatrice came to trial, the drawing might be a help. Maybe the authorities wouldn't consider it of any value, but then again they might. When they found out how literally truthful Pam was. Which

176

they would find out, if they observed her for any length of time.

She folded the picture carefully and tucked it into the pocket where she had put the envelope addressed to Sam. Only the envelope was no longer there.

She searched for it, frantically, in both apron pockets and in the one in her skirt.

It was gone. It must have fallen out somewhere . . . oh, God, what if Beatrice or "Pet" found it? They wouldn't hesitate to open it . . . tampering with other people's mail was the least of their crimes . . . and then what would they do? When they knew she was planning to betray them at the first opportunity?

She made a circuit of the house, as unobtrusively as possible, hoping that it might still lie where it had fallen, but there was no sign of the letter. Whoever had picked it up . . . and someone must have or it would have been still lying on the floor . . . would he be friend or enemy?

No one returned it to her, and she had no way of knowing whether or not "Pet" or Beatrice might have been its finder.

Mrs. Sanding peered at her rather closely when she was carrying in dinner (later Cillay could not have related what they ate) and asked quietly, "Are you feeling unwell, my dear? You're looking sort of peaky."

"I have a headache," she said, stiff-lipped, and not untruthfully.

The old lady's eyes were shrewd. "Well, if there's anything I can do . . . don't hesitate to ask, my dear."

Her kind voice was almost Cillay's undoing; for a moment she considered telling Mrs. Sanding everything and asking her for help and advice.

But she saw Beatrice watching from the dining room doorway, smiled wanly, and murmured only thanks. To involve Mrs. Sanding . . . or any of the others . . . would only endanger them as well as herself, and she had no doubt that Beatrice would deal with any helper without mercy.

Some time during the meal her thoughts began to crystallize. She could not sit and wait, the helpless fly in "Pet's" terrible web, until they were ready to eliminate her. For that, she was increasingly convinced, was what they would have to do. Beatrice simply could not afford to have anyone running around who knew about Mrs. Fontana. Only the fact that she threatened Pam kept Cillay in line now, and they knew it.

They did threaten Pam. And not only, Cillay thought, with the probability of commitment to an institution. When Cillay suggested that her sister help her carry trash out to the incinerator to burn, Beatrice countermanded her.

"It might be better for you to make two trips. I think Pam ought to stay in the house, under the circumstances, don't you?"

Pam had looked from one face to the other, uncomprehending, and Cillay had given in silently, carrying a wastebasket in each arm. She felt Beatrice's presence in the doorway, watching her progress across the yard. Cillay looked up at her after she had dumped the papers and saw the narrow lips twist sardonically. *Go ahead*, she might have been saying. *Run, if you like, but your sister stays here. You can't get her away with you.*

Cillay considered, as dispassionately as she could. If she were to turn to the police . . . take off from here, for instance, running down the alley . . . Beatrice could not stop her. Could not move fast enough to prevent her leaving the back yard, to catch her before she reached a telephone.

But Pam would be left behind. Beatrice had already demonstrated her brutality. That she would hesitate to use it against Pam was most unlikely.

No, if Cillay ran it had to be with her sister, not alone. Which meant that for the time being she could not run.

She stood beside the incinerator, ostensibly to watch the fire, to see that nothing escaped through the screen covering, occasionally poking in a few more handfuls of waste material. She was so close to freedom here . . . only a few steps into the alley-way . . . the thought of going back into the house sent a chill through her, but she knew it was necessary. For now. For now. But Beatrice would not stay awake indefinitely. There must be a time when her guard would drop.

In the meantime, until the chance arose to get Pammy safely away with her, she would do some looking of her own. Not for the money Beatrice and "Pet" were searching for (and Sam? Had he looked for money? Or for evidence against this formidable pair, evidence of some crime of which Cillay was as yet ignorant?) but something to prove that her aunt, Elsa Pomeroy, was not the grossly fat woman who stuffed herself with chocolates and did nothing

179

else. Something to prove what had happened to the real Elsa Pomeroy.

The conviction grew that her aunt was dead. Had they disposed of her, as they had disposed of Mrs. Fontana? Cillay looked about her. Elsa Pomeroy had been alive and in good health a little over three months ago when she had written to them to come. If she had died in the meantime, what had they done with her?

The house was very large, but there was no place where a body could be hidden in it for any period of time. Decomposition would lead a seeker to it within a matter of days. There was no basement under the house, no spot in the minute back yard where the earth had been disturbed by digging . . .

Cillay brought her head around with an audible snap of her neck, then remembered that Beatrice was watching and pretended to have heard something in the alley. *Be careful, be careful, she told herself. She may kill you eventually, anyway, but if she knows you're on to anything she will only do it sooner . . .*

There was no place in the yard which had been dug up. Beatrice could not have risked that, for it would certainly have been noticed by tenants and perhaps by neighbors; in spite of the high fence which surrounded the place those on either side could look down from their second story windows. No, she would not have wanted to risk notice by digging up the back yard when it had obviously been neglected for years.

But there was a place she could have dug, Cillay thought, excitement making her cold and also

180

heightening her perceptivity. The garage had a dirt floor. And no one could possibly have watched had Beatrice wanted to dig there. It had been in semi-darkness when she glanced into it several days previously, and full of odds and ends of debris. How could she get into it to look around?

It was only then, turning with what she hoped was a casual air to look toward the garage, that she saw something new had been added since she had been out here last.

A shiny new padlock secured the double doors.

Chapter 17

Cillay knew, beyond any doubt, that some, if not all, of the answers she sought were there, behind that locked garage door.

She knew, also, that Beatrice would be the one carrying the key and that there was virtually no chance of getting hold of it.

There remained several windows. Even if she were free to wander about in the daytime and look into them, she knew she would see very little. The interior was too dark. But wasn't there a chance she could get in through one of the windows?

She stood at the window of her room that night, looking down onto the back yard. It was only faintly illuminated by lights from the houses on either side; only enough so that she could make out the bulk of the garage at the back of the lot.

She had tried, after Pam was put to bed, to slip out of the house. But Beatrice occupied a seat in the front parlor, where she could watch the front door, and the kitchen door was locked with a key. There was a side door, also, but it could only be reached by passing the doorway of the room where "Pet" sucked her candies before the television screen, and no doubt it, too, was locked with a key which Beatrice kept in her pocket.

The moon, not yet full, was rising over the tops of distant houses, and its pale light touched the edge of the roof outside her room. The third floor was not quite so extensive as the lower floors, and there was an area of roof with a gentle slope away from her windows. Cillay looked at it, her heart beginning to race.

She had been rather good at climbing at one time, although she hadn't tried it for years now. Getting out the window would be easy enough . . . she tried to remember, from her examination of the house this afternoon, what hand and footholds there might be.

The house was a true old Victorian, covered with gingerbread and scrollwork, all of it leaving dozens of indentations and projections. It was, she thought with rising excitement, quite possible that she could get down the back wall of the house without killing herself.

It was also a possibility that she would not be able to get back in again. But if she got out, would that be necessary? If Beatrice didn't know she was gone (and why should she?) there would be no reason to harm Pam. Cillay could investigate the garage, and whether or not she found anything incriminating she could then go to a neighboring house and call the police. They would come back with her and Beatrice would have to open the door to them . . . it would be too late by then for her to do anything about it.

She couldn't try anything without a flashlight. There was one in the kitchen, in a drawer full of junk. It was too early to try for it, for people were still up, but after they'd had time to go to sleep . . .

She made her way, barefooted, down the back stairs and appropriated the flashlight. Its batteries were good; she tried it to see.

There were footsteps . . . she recognized Beatrice's halting steps, for she had once more discarded her crutches . . . along the hallway, and in a flash of panic she put the flashlight inside the stairway, hoping that Beatrice would have no reason to open that door. It was too late to get away without being seen or heard.

Beatrice paused on seeing the kitchen lighted, her eyes going to the locked door to reassure herself that it was still secure. "Oh, it's you. What are you doing down here so late?"

"I . . . thought I'd like something hot to drink. I can't sleep." That was true enough, at any rate.

"Oh. Well, I've been deputized to make a pot of tea for us all. Maybe you'd get down the cups for me while I get the water boiling." Beatrice looked pointedly at her bare feet but made no comment upon them.

Cillay willingly got down cups. Of course, what had she been thinking of? Beatrice had to have sound sleepers again tonight, didn't she? For Mrs. Fontana's body still lay in that upstairs bedroom, and it must be gotten out tonight. Perhaps, she thought, Beatrice would ask for her assistance in moving it; perhaps it would be taken to the garage and she would be asked to help carry it.

She was sick with the thought of lugging poor little Mrs. Fontana about like a sack of feed, but she would do it if it gained her entry into the garage.

Surely she would be able to see something, if she were allowed even a few minutes . . .

She was not invited to do anything, however, but to carry in the tray of tea things. She wondered if the old people were suspicious of Beatrice's generosity, but apparently they were not. It had happened a number of times before, that she felt like offering them a late evening snack or drink, and they were happy to take advantage of it.

Cillay did not see that Beatrice added anything to the tea except for sugar and lemon, but as they all drank it sugared some of her sedative could easily have been added to that ahead of time.

Beatrice poured out the steaming drink and began to serve it. Cillay took a cup of it to Mrs. Sanding, who sat at a card table with her eternal solitaire game. Cillay felt guilty, passing it over; but was it not, after all, better that Mrs. Sanding should sleep through whatever was to happen tonight?

The old lady gave a crow of triumph and slapped a red six down on a black seven, then turned to smile at Cillay. "How nice. Thank you, my dear."

She had to speak, to pretend to normalcy. "Is it sweet enough for you?"

Mrs. Sanding sipped noisily. "Just right, just right."

Cillay forced a grimace that might pass for a smile, wishing that she dared to ask for help, knowing all the while that the old lady was as helpless as she herself.

"Now where's that ace of spades?" the old lady was muttering. "I can't get anywhere without the ace of spades."

"Never mind about the tray and the cups," Beatrice said, crossing toward them. "You can get it in the morning. I know you wanted to go to bed early."

She was glad to escape. Beatrice hadn't tried to give her the quieting drug this evening. Did she think Cillay would be too frightened to venture out of her room, or was she simply indifferent? Knowing, perhaps, that Cillay would never have the opportunity to tell anyone what she knew?

She retrieved the flashlight from the back stairway and climbed to her room. She did not, however, get into bed. Instead, she put on slacks and a dark sweater against the night chill in the house, and sneakers that would be soundless, she hoped, on the stairs, and went to see what she could see of Beatrice's activities.

The back stairs, with a landing on the second floor, were totally dark, which was fine. She could sit on the landing, able to hear anyone coming from below in time to move higher if necessary, able to see the length of the second floor corridor without herself being seen.

She waited a long time, so long that in spite of being uncomfortable and frightened she began to nod. The old people all came up by ten, and within half an hour had all settled down for the night. Lights out, radios off, all movement ceasing. If only Sam were there in his room in the middle of the house, she thought longingly. But Sam was in Atlanta, and the note she had written to him was missing.

The heat had been turned off and as the house cooled it began to creak. Several times Cillay thought she heard someone on the stairs below her and crouched, ready to move, for minutes before realizing that it was only the ancient wood protesting the change of temperature.

And then, when she had nodded so that her neck snapped painfully, she heard Beatrice on the front stairs. A Beatrice walking easily, with scarcely a trace of a limp, although her ankle was still bandaged. The hall was dim, with only one small bulb in the entire length of it, but she was clearly visible. Fitting a key into the lock of Mrs. Fontana's room.

Cillay held her breath, waiting. In almost indecent haste, the door reopened, and Beatrice backed out, dragging a white wrapped burden along the floor. She had rolled the body up in the bedspread and moved quickly, unhesitatingly.

This way . . . she was dragging it this way . . . Cillay began to uncoil her legs, preparatory to moving. She hadn't, somehow, considered that Beatrice would take the body out this way . . . the stairs were so narrow and dark. They were also, of course, much more private, in case anyone hadn't gotten enough of that tea to put them to sleep for the night.

But before Cillay had time to do more than creep cautiously up a step or two Beatrice stopped. There was a small door set into the wall, a door Cillay had assumed opened into a linen closet or storage area. Beatrice pulled the door wide open and stopped again to tug her bundle into position, then struggled briefly to force it into the opening.

A moment later she straightened, closed the door, and moved rapidly toward Cillay.

It was too late to move. She could only press herself against the wall, trusting that the darkness was

187

deep enough to hide her, as Beatrice passed within a few feet of her.

She experimented with a few deep breaths as she listened to Beatrice's receding feet below. Even after she heard the door close at the foot of the stairs it was several minutes before she felt enough in control to move out and investigate the compartment into which Mrs. Fontana's body had been placed.

A laundry chute. No wonder Beatrice hadn't needed help. And how foolish of her to wince, thinking of that body hitting the bottom of the chute. Mrs. Fontana was long past the point where she needed sympathy. All she needed now, Cillay thought, was justice . . . having her murderer brought to account. If only it were possible to do it without implicating Pam!

She made her way back to her darkened room and stood again at the window, straining to see down into the yard. The moon was all the way up, now, but there were patches of cloud that cut it off spasmodically. And then there was a space of open sky and for a period of several minutes the scene below was flooded with a pale light.

Beatrice, dragging her white bundle across the yard toward the garage. That had to be where she was going with it, and Cillay watched in a state beyond horror until the woman vanished around the edge of the building.

Too late, it occurred to her that she might have gotten out of the house while Beatrice was engaged in her grisly task, for she must have left the back door open, must she not, until she could return to the house herself? But already Beatrice was coming back . . .

188

she had not buried the body, then, only gotten it out of the house.

How could she be standing here, watching a mad woman dispose of the body of an innocent old woman, and contemplating her own escape? So calmly, so quietly. For, outwardly, she was quiet. Her hands, although cold, did not tremble. Her breathing had steadied to a nearly normal rate.

Again she waited. The house was still. Had Beatrice been able to go to bed and to sleep, undisturbed by the events of the past twenty-four hours?

Cillay herself had never felt less sleepy. After a full hour had passed and nothing, so far as she knew, had moved in the house she got up and went to the window.

She would have preferred having a rope to hang over the edge of the roof; it would have been a safety factor. The house was high, built with fourteen foot ceilings in the manner of Victorian houses; if she slipped, it was a long way to the ground. Possibly a fatally long way.

But she couldn't wait. Without knowing Beatrice's plans, she had no way of knowing her chances of getting through another day without some irrevocable action on the part of those two women. She had to go now.

The window opened noisily and she waited again, her heart rate speeding up. She could not lock her door, for if there had been a key to it Beatrice had confiscated it that first night. She put a chair under the knob of the door, and the same in the room where Pam slept soundly, and flipped the lock on the bathroom door, too. At best it would slow them down a little, if they tried to check on her. She didn't think they would. Beatrice had moved calmly, unhurriedly, in disposing of the body, confident that she was unwatched. Why should she worry now, when she had obviously made certain that none of the doors or windows on the lower floor could be opened? Except for the window in Aunt Elsa's room . . . no, "Pet's" room . . . the screens were securely in place, almost impossible to move without a racket. Besides, even the first floor windows were far enough from the ground to make a jump dangerous.

No matter. Don't think about any of that now. Just think about getting down. Cillay lifted a leg over the window sill and tested the roof of the back part of the house. Perfectly sound. As solid as when the house was built, some seventy years ago.

She had tied a belt around the end of the flashlight . . . fortunately it was one of those with a flaring bulb end . . . and knotted it to the back of her own belt, where it bumped awkwardly against her behind.

She visualized again the back of the house as she had seen it during her inspection earlier in the day. At the corners were intricately fashioned decorative strips that should offer plenty of holes for her feet and hands . . .

She stood for a moment on the edge of the roof, glad it was too dark to see clearly how far away the ground was. Then she dropped flat on her stomach and swung a leg over, searching for the toe holds that ought to be there. The roofing was rough and scratched her stomach where her shirt pulled loose, but she ignored it. For a few seconds her foot encountered only air and panic surged . . .

"Take it easy," she whispered. "You just haven't slid far enough over the edge . . ."

The trouble was there was nothing more than the edge of the roof itself, with a metal gutter that might or might not be strong enough to support her weight, to hold onto while she went over the edge.

There. Her foot touched wood, poked about, found a hole that was large enough to admit it. She tested it, gingerly, then risked the gutter and felt with the other foot.

The gutter held, although for a few alarming seconds it seemed that it might pull loose. And then she was below it, hands gripping the carvings, not so easily as she had hoped because the design was large rather than fine, and her hands were too small to close around the sections . . . but hanging on, moving steadily downward, for what seemed an age . . . until her feet encountered bushes at the bottom and she pushed herself outward and jumped.

She landed sprawling, the flashlight digging into her flesh, and sat for a moment, shaking, now that she had done it.

The house was dark, as were the houses on both sides. Where should she go, at this time of night, to call the police? The nearest pay phone she knew about was some four blocks away and she shrank from covering that distance, at night, alone. Yet she shrank even more from reentering that terrible house.

But first the garage, she thought. Not that Mrs. Fontana's body wasn't evidence enough for the police. But if she could find some trace of her aunt . . . if she could prove to the authorities immediately that "Pet" was not Elsa Pomeroy . . . perhaps Pam could be kept out of things altogether.

She dusted off her slacks and her hands and moved purposefully toward the garage. The padlock, as she had expected, was in place and secure. There was no getting in that way, not without the key.

She chose the window on the far side of the building, the one which could not be seen from the house. Disappointingly, it resisted all her efforts; it must be fastened on the inside.

Cillay paused for a moment, trying to decide whether it was worth the risk of breaking a window or whether she'd be far wiser to go immediately to a telephone. And it was then, standing at the side of the garage in the nighttime silence, that she heard it.

Within the outbuilding, someone moaned.

The hair rose, prickling, on her scalp.

Mrs. Fontana was dead . . . she had to be dead.

A moment later the sound was repeated. She moved in, pressing her face against the window, shining the light within. It was of little use; the window was long unwashed, and the beam of the flash not powerful enough to cut through it clearly. It touched upon the open space of hard packed dirt but failed to illuminate the objects on the far side of the building.

"Who's there?" Her whisper seemed to hang on the air; she was afraid to speak loudly for fear of being heard from the house. "Is someone hurt?"

There was no reply. Cillay shifted position,

swiveling the light downward at as sharp an angle as she could manage, her cheek against the cold glass, and this time she was rewarded.

She saw the face, white except where it was streaked with dirt, the thick fair hair falling forward over it, a band of dirty rag tied over the mouth. The eyes were open, staring up at her . . . live eyes, moving eyes, she thought.

She had found him. She had found Alan.

Finding bodies was one thing. Finding a live and possibly injured Alan was another. She turned, knowing she had wasted too much time already. She would get the police immediately, and let them deal with the problem of getting into the building.

She heard the crackle of a twig, broken under an incautious foot, but it was too late. Before she could swing her light around, before she could so much as open her mouth in a scream that might rouse a neighbor, she was struck on the back of the head and went down in a red haze of pain.

Chapter 18

She was not knocked out, but the agony of the injury was, for a few minutes, incapacitating. She knew, vaguely, that hands were pulling at her . . . dragging her, as Mrs. Fontana had been dragged . . . and that someone was mouthing obscenities over her.

Beatrice. As the pain receded enough so that her mind began to function once more, Cillay knew that it was Beatrice who had jerked her hands behind her and secured them with a length of rope that cut into her flesh. Beatrice who tossed her carelessly into a corner of the garage on the hard packed earth floor, next to something smelling of gasoline and some hard sacks that might have contained cement or feed. She was in an awkward and painful position, and her head ached all the way down into her neck and shoulders. She saw, when Beatrice flashed the light around for a final inspection, the instrument with which she had been struck. A hammer, its heavy head stained with blood, dropped onto the ground beside her.

The light swung toward her face, blinding her. Cillay could not see Beatrice behind it, but the voice was familiar enough. "You couldn't leave well enough alone, could you? Well, don't complain now if you have to pay the price for your nosiness."

She had killed Mrs. Fontana . . . struck her in

the chest with the scissors . . . that was all Cillay could think of. And her aunt . . . Elsa Pomeroy . . . what had they done to her? And Alan . . . she remembered, now, she had seen Alan's face . . . Alan's eyes open and moving . . .

She twisted against the ropes that restrained her wrists and ankles, trying to see across the garage. There was too little light, she couldn't make out anything.

Beatrice thought she was trying to escape. "Struggle, for all the good it will do you. By the time I fix a gag over your mouth you'll be just as helpless as he is."

"Who are you?" Cillay whispered, turning her head to avoid the blinding light.

"What does it matter? You'll never tell anyone about me."

"What have you done with my aunt?"

Beatrice had started to turn away; she paused, now, and when she aimed the light to the side Cillay could see her face, the over-large nose, the hooded eyes. When she spoke her voice was softer.

"So you know about that, do you? How did you find out?"

There was a creaking sound as the door swung open; Beatrice, startled, spun about with her flashlight, pinpointing the squat, obese figure of "Pet." She had not undressed for bed, although it must be three in the morning by now. She was panting with the exertion of having come down the steps and across the yard, and her voice was shrill.

"What's happened? Was it her? Beatrice . . ."

She stopped when the revealing light beam touched Cillay briefly, then swung to neutral ground between them.

"How did she get out? You said she couldn't, the doors were locked . . ."

"Well, I saw her, didn't I? So stop fussing. She climbed out a window. How could I know she'd be fool enough to try that?"

"But she might have gotten to the police! You said . . ."

"Oh, for God's sake, shut up!" Beatrice spat, whirling on her co-conspirator. "She didn't get away. She's right here, so don't panic!"

From the shadows on the far side of the building there was a rustling sound and someone moaned. Alan, Cillay thought. He must be hurt.

"What's that?" "Pet" stood rigidly, just inside the double doors, her face a lump of suet in the feeble illumination. "Good God, who . . . !"

"It's Alan," Cillay said. "He's hurt, he needs a doctor . . ."

The fat woman fixed her small, dark eyes on Beatrice. "But you said he had left . . . you said . . ."

"I didn't see any reason to upset you," Beatrice said, her voice suddenly smooth, conciliating. "He was snooping around . . . I caught him out here, he'd come home early that day and I couldn't let him poke around in here, could I?"

"But what are we going to do with them?" Panic sent "Pet's" voice rising until Beatrice took a step toward her, patting her shoulder. "It's one thing to dispose of old ladies who have no one to check on

them, but we can't get away with killing these two
. . . they're young, they'll be missed . . ."

"Who's going to check on this one?" Beatrice
asked, nudging Cillay with one foot. "Oh, don't get
excited. We don't have to kill them, only keep them
here for a few days until we can clear out."

"Clear out?" The older woman's echo rose in a
shriek. "But I don't want to clear out, you idiot! I
want this house, a comfortable living in my old age!
That's all I've ever wanted, the house and the money
it brings in! Now you've messed things up so that
we'll never get them straightened out . . . Why
couldn't you leave well enough alone, we had
the house, and the money will turn up . . . I never
intended to get mixed up in a murder . . . !"

"Well, you're in it, now, just as deep as I am," Beatrice informed her. "And if you don't lower your
voice the neighbors will think there's a murder going
on right now! Don't panic. All we have to do is find
the rest of the money and get out. Someone will find
them; they'll be all right." She dismissed Cillay and
Alan contemptuously.

"But we can't go! All we have is the ten thousand
you took from Mrs. Fontana! That isn't enough to
do anything with! We've never found that wretched
Elsa Pomeroy's hoard . . . oh!" She stopped, gaz-
ing down at the girl lying helpless in the dirt.

"It doesn't matter, she knows you aren't her aunt,"
Beatrice said dispassionately. "She's been snooping
too, I shouldn't wonder. Well, the money has got to
be in that house somewhere, and we'll find it. There
aren't many places left to search. It's only a matter

of days, and it has to turn up. Granted it won't be as much as we'd hoped . . . but we can try to get the balance out of the bank, there's still some left in the other account. You've got the signature down, haven't you? And it's a big bank, chances are no one will know what Elsa Pomeroy is supposed to look like . . ."

"But it's taking such a chance . . ." The fat bosom heaved in agitation. "It would have been different, if I could have withdrawn it a little at a time . . . They're bound to be suspicious, if I take out the entire amount at one time . . ."

"*She* took everything out of the other one, didn't she? Besides, there's no choice, now. You can either try for it all at once, or give it up. That's up to you. *I* can't forge her signature, so the bank book is of no use to me. We can settle for what we already have, and run."

"But it isn't enough! I wanted a safe place to spend the rest of my time . . . this house, and the roomers paying for everything! That's what we agreed upon . . . if only you hadn't lost your head and killed her! There was no need to kill her!"

"Wasn't there? Well, I thought there was. She had the money right there, and she said she'd changed her mind. She wasn't going to pay for the jewelry. I think she suspected something, although I don't know why she should have . . . It's perfectly good stuff. At least *she* always talked about it as if it were genuine and valuable."

She, Cillay thought, feeling the cold of the ground seeping through her clothes and the painfully tight bonds on her wrists. Aunt Elsa . . . they were trying to sell her jewelry to Mrs. Fontana.

"All right, so she refused to buy it. That was no reason to kill her! We could have figured out some other way to get the money . . ."

"She knew I'd taken that ring of hers," Beatrice said, her tone suddenly cold. "She knew you'd made me put it back, but she charged me with it. Threatened me, even, suggested I'd stolen the other stuff, too. What did you expect me to do, wait for her to call in the authorities?"

"You botched up everything! Everything! All we had to do was wait until she died, and we'd have had everything, the same as we got . . . hers."

"Only we didn't get *hers*, remember? She took it out of the bank and hid it somewhere . . . and the rest of it is still in the bank, out of reach unless you're brave enough to walk in and ask for it. Don't blame it all on me, Pet; you've been right along with me, all the way."

"Pet" was near tears, but Cillay found it difficult to stir up any sympathy for her. "But I never intended to get mixed up in any killing . . . only taking the house and the money, and she didn't need it any longer . . . I didn't know she had any relatives, she never mentioned any . . ."

Cillay's lips moved again. "What did you do to her? My aunt? Did you kill her, the way you did Mrs. Fontana?"

"No! No, we never touched her! She died, a heart attack it must have been, and we thought . . . we thought there was no one to know! Only the other

199

roomers, and Beatrice got rid of them, and they knew the old woman was sick, so they thought it was all right . . . All I wanted was a home, a little income so I didn't have to depend on that miserable pension check . . . always skimping, doing without . . . I never planned on murder, that was Beatrice's idea! And now what are we going to do?"

"Well, for one thing we can go in the house and discuss it where it's comfortable," Beatrice decided. "I need something to gag her with, or she'll be screaming down the neighborhood. Have you got anything on you I can use?"

"Pet" pawed about her obese person and came forth with a handkerchief; Beatrice added one of her own stockings to it, to hold the handkerchief in place. Cillay fought against it, for the smell of it carried the stale, unpleasant reminder of "Pet's" person upon it and for a moment she gagged and choked against rising vomit. By sheer will power she forced herself not to vomit; she would only strangle herself if she could not control it. The linen square was pushed between her teeth and the nylon stocking tied over it, the knot making an uncomfortable lump behind her left ear.

The two women stood over her for a moment, making sure she was unable to move or speak. The fat one worked her hands together nervously. "I want one thing understood," she said; she was trying for forcefulness and succeeded only in sounding tremulously frightened. "No more killing. Leave them here, if that's the only thing to do . . . but no more killing. The boy, especially, will be missed. Someone will be looking for him."

"No more killing," Beatrice agreed, but Cillay was looking straight up into the black eyes and she shivered, for she read no confirmation of that statement in them.

"What about the other one? The half wit?"

"What about her? She won't cause any trouble. We'll just leave her here with the old people when we leave. She doesn't know anything; she can't give us away when the police are finally called in."

But we can, Cillay thought. Alan and I. And she can't afford to leave us here, alive to talk to the police. Can she?

They were going, locking the padlock, leaving Cillay and Alan in darkness. Alan made no sounds, now. She was afraid he had lapsed into unconsciousness, and for a while she wished that she, too, might take that easy way out.

Chapter 19

For a long time she did not try to move, beyond wriggling into a position which was slightly more comfortable. Tears flooded her eyes but she resolutely fought them back; crying while gagged is a risky proposition at best. Once Beatrice and "Pet" had gone the darkness seemed absolute, the silence intense. Gradually Cillay became aware of the sound of breathing . . . Alan's breathing. Rather louder than normal, she decided. How badly was he hurt? If only Sam had consented to investigate . . .

But Sam had not, and he was in Atlanta, and who knew when he would return?

If it were only a matter of days, if Beatrice found the money she was seeking or decided to leave without it, chances are they would survive here without difficulty, although they might lose a few pounds and would be pretty much of a mess when found. For they would be found, Cillay assured herself. Beatrice might palm off on the roomers another story of illness, but once she and "Pet" had gone they would come looking for her. Surely they would do that.

Cillay went over and over the situation in her mind, staring up into the darkness. She tried to take courage from "Pet's" insistence on no more violence, but this was hard to do. She knew that "Pet" could not stop Beatrice from whatever action she considered necessary, and it was not only possible but probable that she would feel Cillay knew too much to be allowed to live. Time after time the picture of Mrs. Fontana came to her mind, chest soaked with blood, sliding down the side of her bed, carrying the spread with her . . . Cillay felt the cold sweat break out on her own body.

Yet she had not killed Alan. Injured him in some way, obviously, or she could not have overpowered him. But she had then bound and gagged him, not killed him. Didn't that indicate that she was truly going along with the policy of no more killing? And they would have to run soon, if they hoped to escape, for Alan's disappearance could not pass unnoticed for long. He had a family, and he was enrolled in college where someone must eventually wonder what had happened to him.

Would someone come seeking him in time, though? For he was injured. How badly? If only he could speak to her . . .

She tried to remember what obstacles there were in the middle of the garage, between herself and Alan. Most of the junk was at the sides and rear of the single room. Perhaps she could roll over to him, although what good that would do she hadn't yet figured out. However, to do anything was better than to lie here waiting for Beatrice to come back and put an end to them.

Rolling was awkward and painful, but not impossible. She had to maneuver around a shovel that had been dropped . . . had it been used to dig her aunt's grave, and waited now to dig Mrs. Fontana's? . . . but there was nothing else to impede her progress.

It had taken some time, for the sky was a pale gray beyond the dirty glass of the windows when she came up against the bulk that was Alan. He had been covered with an old Army blanket, probably more to disguise his shape than to keep him warm. Was it only the pale light, or was his skin also grayish in tone?

He lay quietly, only the sound of his breathing betraying life. If only she could work this gag loose to speak to him . . . would he be able to respond? Or was he in deep shock or coma?

Beatrice had done her job too well; Cillay could find nothing on which to catch the sturdy nylon that held her gag in place, and it was too tight to rub it free otherwise.

She gave up after a time, lying quietly beside Alan, grateful at least that he was warm and still breathing.

She would not have believed it possible to sleep under these conditions, but she did. She woke with a start at the sound of a key being fitted into the padlock, and blinked against the bright sunlight streaming in through the doorway. She had slept for hours, it seemed, in what must have been sheer exhaustion, for every bone and muscle ached.

Beatrice bent over her, whipping off the stocking and allowing her to spit out the gag. Her voice was low but vicious. "All right, where is she?"

Cillay stared at her, uncomprehending. The fat woman pretending to be Elsa Pomeroy had entered the garage, too, and was pulling the door shut behind her.

204

"What did she say?" "Pet" panted. "How did she get her out of the house?"

"She hasn't said anything yet. But she will." Beatrice kicked out at her, brutally, unexpectedly, striking Cillay in the ribs so that she was unable to control the cry forced from her lips. "Where is she?"

"Who?" Her mouth was dry and her ribs hurt; it was all she could do to speak. "I don't know what you mean."

"Your sister! What have you done with her? How did you get her out of the house?"

"Pam? Pam's . . . gone?"

Beatrice kicked her again, with more feeling this time, and watched coldly while the girl on the ground squirmed in agony. "You know damn well she's gone. How did you do it? Where is she?"

Cillay flopped her head once in negation. "I don't . . . know! Please . . . I don't know!"

"She must know," "Pet" stated anxiously. "Make her tell, Beatrice."

Cillay tried to curl her body against the toe of that sturdy shoe but it did not come again.

"Maybe she doesn't know," Beatrice concluded reluctantly. "Not that I'd mind kicking it out of her, if necessary. But maybe she really doesn't know."

"But what if she's pretending? What if the girl is telling someone about us, right now? We've got to know where she is, who she went to!"

"The girl's an idiot. She won't tell anyone much of anything. Maybe she just wandered off, when her sister wasn't there to get her up and around this morning." Beatrice stared at her broodingly, the hooded dark eyes like those of a bird of prey.

Pam was gone. Cillay was too stunned, momentarily, to worry about what they were going to do with her. Pam would never have wandered out of the house alone. She seldom did anything unless she was told to do it. To leave a house, on her own, in unfamiliar territory such as this, was completely out of character.

"But we can't be sure," the fat woman said; fear literally dribbled from her mouth.

"Well, what do you want me to do?" Beatrice demanded, exasperated. "I can kick her until she's unconscious, and that won't make her tell if she doesn't know. We'd be better off looking for the money, and then when we find it we'll get the hell out of here."

"Please . . ." Cillay twisted her head to see both their faces. "Alan's badly hurt . . . His breathing doesn't sound right. He needs a doctor."

"That's his tough luck," Beatrice commented. "Serves him right for snooping where he doesn't belong. Who is he, anyway? Why was he spying on us?"

"I don't know. But it will be murder if he dies . . ."

Beatrice laughed, and Cillay had never heard so unpleasant a sound. "So what's one more? Come on, Pet, let's stuff the gag back in her mouth and get back into the house. You'll have to cope with meals today and I'll go over the place again; that money has got to turn up, and fast."

If only she could free her hands and feet, Cillay thought desperately. If she could surprise Beatrice the next time she came, or . . .

"Please . . . couldn't you let me loose long enough to . . . to go to the bathroom?"

"And try some other little trick at the same time? You're as big a fool as your sister. Here, Pet, cram that rag in her mouth while I tie it . . ."

Cillay could have shot herself for what happened then. If only she'd been able to conceal her emotions, the hope and joy that must have been written across her face, they wouldn't have noticed anything.

They were both bent over her when she saw the face at the window. Little old Mrs. Sanding, face pressed against the glass, shielding her eyes from the sun with both hands, looking directly down into Cillay's face.

Beatrice jerked back with an oath, and Mrs. Sanding wasn't quite quick enough to drop out of sight. "Pet" stared, open-mouthed, then demanded shrilly, "Catch her, Beatrice, stop her!"

It's broad daylight, Cillay thought, Beatrice can't do anything to her in daylight, with people in the houses on both sides of us . . .

Anyone seeing the brief struggle between the frail old lady and the younger, stronger woman might have had the decency to call the police. But the fences were high, and no one was looking down into the yard. No one saw, no one called, no one came. Beatrice was breathing rather heavily, but she managed it without much difficulty, thrusting Mrs. Sanding ahead of her through the doorway.

"Pet" was making moaning noises. "Now what are we going to do? Oh, my God, you've spoiled everything! If you'd let me do it the way I wanted, no one would have been hurt and we could have stayed here forever . . . !"

Mrs. Sanding darted forward, oblivious of her own

danger, to stoop beside Cillay. "Oh, you poor thing! Have they hurt you?"

"Alan's hurt . . . He's unconscious," Cillay told her painfully. She wondered if her own ribs were broken or only bruised.

And then Beatrice jerked Mrs. Sanding to her feet and swung her around; it seemed as if she might strike her, but instead she fought to keep her temper under control.

"What are you doing, snooping around?"

"I wondered what was going on," Mrs. Sanding admitted candidly. "Mrs. Fontana carried off to the hospital in the middle of the night, you said, and then Cillay missing, and such a rotten breakfast . . . Never could abide your cooking." She was quite calm. "I saw you out here, and Mrs. Pomeroy following you . . . thought it was strange, to say the least."

"You should have minded your own business," Beatrice said through her teeth. "Now that you're here, you'll have to stay here."

The thin white eyebrows rose. "What, another disappearance? Alan, and Mrs. Fontana, and Cillay, and now me? What are you going to do about Elizabeth and Mr. Gary? Are they going to disappear, too? You don't think they're fools, do you? That they'll accept your cockeyed explanations?"

They were frozen for a moment, all looking at one another, no one speaking. Then "Pet" moistened her fat lips and whispered, "What do you mean?"

"I mean I knew you put something into my tea last night to make me sleep . . . and into everyone else's, as well. And that you've had this poor child terrorized for days . . . She's a regular little ghost with those big dark eyes in a white face . . . and you're flying around in a desperate hurry about something. What is it?" When she received no answer to her query, she spoke to Cillay. "What's really happened to Mrs. Fontana?"

"She's dead," Cillay said before anyone could stop her. "She's . . . over there, wrapped in a bedspread."

Mrs. Sanding's eyes widened, but she nodded. "I suspected something nasty. What rot, to expect us to believe we'd all slept through an ambulance coming to take her away . . . How did she die?"

"Beatrice stabbed her with the scissors."

Beatrice made a convulsive movement. "I! Why, you wretched little fool; you know it was your sister who did it! You saw the scissors in her bedroom, and the blood on her clothes . . . !"

Cillay did not reply, watching Mrs. Sanding's face, and the old woman nodded. "I see. So now what is your brilliant plan?" She swiveled toward Beatrice. "Mass murders? I guess you figured out some way to explain Mrs. Fontana, but all the rest of us? It won't matter how fast you go or how far you run, they'll find you, you know. If you kill all of us. One accident, yes, but accidents to all of us?" Incredibly, she chuckled. "Oh, you must be quite a plotter, Beatrice, but that will take some real plotting!"

"Accidents happen in old houses," Beatrice said icily. "Fires, in old wooden buildings. Starting in the middle of the night, all the old people burned to death, young girl sleeping on the top floor . . .

trapped there. Happens every once in a while. House is destroyed before anyone sees the fire and calls in an alarm."

The erstwhile Elsa Pomeroy gave a little shriek. "But we can't burn the house . . . the money is hidden in it, somewhere!"

"We'll find the money, first. Or if we can't, it will have to burn up with them. What good is it, if we can't take it with us? And we've got to go . . . tonight. We don't dare stay any longer."

Tonight. And Sam was still in Atlanta, and she hadn't managed to mail the note to him . . . but Pam was gone. If the house burned around their heads, at least Pam wouldn't be in it, for what comfort that was. If only she knew what had happened to her! Wherever she was, she was no doubt better off than if she'd remained here . . .

"We're wasting time when we could be looking for the money," Beatrice said sharply. "Come on, let's get them tied and gagged and not worry about them. We can take them back into the house when it's dark."

The gag was stuffed back into Cillay's mouth, smothering her outcries, and another improvised for Mrs. Sanding. The old lady took it with reasonably good grace and was left sitting upright against one of the bags of feed or fertilizer or whatever they were. Cillay tried to convey a message with her eyes . . . *I'm sorry*.

No sooner had the lock been snapped back onto the doors, however, than Mrs. Sanding flopped over and began to wriggle awkwardly but fairly rapidly across the dirt floor. Cillay watched her hopefully, for there was purpose in her action.

It was light, now, for with the bright sunshine even the dirty windows didn't keep out the illumination. It was possible to make out the shapes of garden tools in a far corner, and it was toward these that Mrs. Sanding made her way.

Interest stirred in Cillay, quite apart from their present predicament. Half-hidden under old gunny sacks was a motorcycle. Did Beatrice ride it? Was this how she had followed them to the carnival in the hope of getting Cillay out of her way?

Cillay could not follow all the old lady's gyrations, but she heard the clattering of metal on metal and some subdued grunting, and suddenly Mrs. Sanding's hands were free. She sat up, sawing on the flimsy rope that held her ankles with a large pair of pruning shears.

It was, after that, only a matter of minutes before she had pulled loose her own gag and bent over Cillay to strip away the offending stocking.

"There! My, how handy to keep the pruning shears down low enough for me to reach them!" She surveyed her wrists, which she had punctured in a few places while freeing them. "I suppose I'll need a tetanus shot, won't I? Worry about that after we get out of here. Are you all right?"

"Bruised, that's all. She kicked me," Cillay sat up and held out her hands behind her until she felt the pressure give way as the rope fragments dropped off. Strangely, her wrists were more painful now than they had been while tied; she sat massaging them while the inexplicable old lady freed her feet.

"Now what about that poor boy?"

It was easy to see what had happened to him. A

nasty laceration, as Mrs. Sanding said, about his right temple. It ought to have been sutured and it looked as if it were becoming infected.

"Stupid woman. Probably hit him with something filthy. Your head has bled, too, did you know? Not that it matters, a little blood. Boy, Alan, can you hear me?"

Alan moved, moaning slightly in response to their hands upon him, but didn't open his eyes.

"We've got to get him to a doctor," Cillay said. "I wonder if those windows can be opened from the inside?"

They inspected the one over Alan's head, and found that it had never been intended to open at all.

"We could break it," Cillay said uncertainly. "But unless we can break out those inner wooden strips we wouldn't be able to get through it."

"Maybe we'd better watch for someone to come along the alley, and then break it and yell to them to get help," Mrs. Sanding suggested. "They aren't going to roast us until tonight, so we've got a little time yet."

It was amazing, how much better she felt, having her mouth and hands free; and Mrs. Sanding's attitude was infecting her. She flashed the old lady a smile, her first genuine one in some time. "It's a dirt floor. Maybe we could tunnel underneath the wall. There's a shovel somewhere . . ."

"Ha, good idea! Let's try that! Or first maybe we ought to consider how we'll cope with that Beatrice if she comes back unexpectedly . . . what is there to hit her over the head with?" She had wandered back to the far corner where the tools were heaped; she came back with a small sledge hammer. "I don't know if I could swing that, but maybe you can. I think the pruning shears might make a formidable weapon, and I can heft those. I guess she'd need a tetanus shot, too, but I'm not sure I care about that."

Cillay almost laughed at that. "I'll tell you what. I'll start digging, on this side of the garage. Can you see the back steps from the other window? So you can watch and warn me if they're coming back?"

"Certainly. When you get tired we'll change about. My lord, I haven't shoveled anything in thirty years! Well, I can't think of a time when I had more incentive . . ."

Chapter 20

She posted herself at the window to watch the house, and Cillay began to dig. It was harder than she'd anticipated. The ground was the consistancy of cement, and the shovel was old and dull. Nevertheless, it was the best hope they had, and she bent to it, chipping away the earth, little by little.

Suddenly remembering, she straightened and turned toward her companion. "Mrs. Sanding . . . They said Pam was missing. Do you have any idea what happened to her? It's not at all like her to wander off on her own . . ."

Unexpectedly, Mrs. Sanding began to laugh. In fact, she laughed so hard that Cillay thought for a moment that it was all too much for her, that she was hysterical.

"Oh, yes, I know!" she chortled. "I wish Beatrice could hear it, too . . . not that she'd appreciate it, I suppose . . . no sense of humor, that woman. I always say there's something odd about a person with no sense of humor. Oh, oh, it *was* funny!"

Cillay waited for her to stifle her amusement, continuing to pick away at the earth. Mrs. Sanding shifted her position so as to have the best view of the house and related her story without taking her eyes off the back steps.

"I knew there was something fishy going on . . . I knew when I woke up this morning she'd put something into the tea again. Happened a couple of times before . . . Whatever were they doing, that they had to have us all sleeping so soundly?"

"Looking for some money they think is hidden in the house. What happened to Pam?"

"Oh, she's all right. Far better off than we are, at the moment, believe me. Well, I didn't swallow that story about Mrs. Fontana being rushed off to the hospital, either . . . I tried to get into her room and it was locked. And then we got downstairs and she brought us those dreadful pancakes . . . I think she's too stingy to use milk with the mix, and water always makes them so leathery . . . and she didn't put in the bit of buckwheat like you do, either. Anyway, she said you were sick, and your sister looked up and said 'oh,' so that was the first she'd heard of it, and I thought it was coming a bit strong . . . Mrs. Fontana sick with her door locked, you sick and out of sight . . . I hadn't missed the way you'd been looking, scared to death. Well, after breakfast I slipped upstairs to see for myself and you were gone, and I'll be darned if it didn't look as if you'd gone out the window!"

She looked at Cillay across the garage. "Did you? Climb down the back of the house?"

"Yes." This was going to take too long; she looked around for another tool and found a pry bar. Yes, she could chip better with that than with the shovel.

"I like a girl with gumption," Mrs. Sanding asserted. "I'd have done it, at your age. In fact, I guess I'd try it now, if that witch was burning the house down around me. Anyway, I didn't know

what was going on . . . still don't . . . but I figured it was something bad. I knew you wouldn't have
left without your sister unless it was. And I figured
you'd want her out of there, too, if it could be done."

"Was it you who got her out?" Cillay stopped picking, and the old lady waved a hand to get her started
again.

"Yes. Oh, did I ever get her out! Right under Beatrice's nose, and she never knew it! Oh, it was priceless!"

"How? She wouldn't have let you . . ."

"Oh, heavens, no, I knew that! So I told her Elizabeth . . . Miss Appleton . . . had neuralgia, that
her face was hurting something awful and that she
wanted me to take her to the doctor's to get something
for it. She couldn't have cared less about anyone else's
neuralgia, naturally. I called a cab, right in front of
her, said I wanted one to take us over to the Medical Center. Then I went up and got your sister . . .
biddable little girl, isn't she? Does just what you tell
her, no more, no less. It was enough. I got into Elizabeth's room while she was taking a bath . . . a dirty
trick, I suppose, but after all it was important . . .
and walked off with that flowered coat she has, and
her wig!"

"Her wig! Good grief, you made Beatrice think
Pam was Miss Appleton?"

"Yes! Yes, yes! Put the wig on her, and the coat
covered everything but her shoes . . . good thing
Beatrice didn't look at her shoes. I told her to hold a
scarf over her face, as if she were in pain, and keep
her eyes down . . . those brown eyes would never
have passed for blue . . . and Beatrice was in such

a state over whatever's going on that she never knew the difference! She was standing right there in the front hall when I marched the girl down, right past her, and out the front door to the taxi! Oh, I tell you, it was priceless!"

"But where did you take her? Where is she? I thought you didn't have any more friends in this place than I have . . ."

"I don't know much of anybody. The only thing I could think of . . . well, you trust that Sam Chellmand, don't you?"

Something twisted, painfully, in her chest. "Yes. I should have trusted him sooner, and we wouldn't be in this mess."

"I don't know what he was here for, either. He wasn't a rooming house type, but if he was anti-Beatrice I figured he was on our side. So I did the same thing you did, I expect . . . looked him up in the phone book and gave the cab driver his home address. That's where she is, all safe and sound."

"But he isn't there . . . he's in Atlanta . . ."

"Yes, but Mrs. Chellmand was there. I explained to her . . . just a little, she's a sensible woman, thank God, for I couldn't have explained very much . . . and she said not to worry, that she'd see Pam was all right. Lovely woman. Very fond of Mr. Chellmand, apparently. She said she'd do whatever he would want done. So that's where she is, and Beatrice hasn't a hope of finding her."

Her relief in knowing Pam was safe was almost wiped out by the terrible constriction in her chest. *Mrs. Chellmand.*

How could she have been so stupid, not to have realized there might be a Mrs. Chellmand.

But he hadn't mentioned a wife . . . and he had kissed her. Her body flooded with warmth, her eyes with tears, remembering how he had kissed her.

Blinded, she poked viciously at the hard-packed earth with the iron pry bar. Well, she hadn't gotten to be nineteen years old without learning that men sometimes kiss pretty girls even when they have wives. Only it hadn't occurred to her that he might be married . . . She wouldn't have dreamed it could hurt so much to learn that.

"It was a dirty trick to pull on poor Elizabeth," Mrs. Sanding was going on, her amusement bubbling through. "She couldn't go out of her room without her wig . . . Couldn't even open the door to ask someone to bring her a tray . . . I suspect she'd starve to death before letting anyone see her without that absurd thing on her head. I brought it back, naturally . . . Mrs. Chellmand gave me a paper bag to carry it in; she thought it was quite funny, too . . . and I knocked and left it outside Elizabeth's door. Didn't have the courage to stay until she opened the door. I suppose she'd like to tear me limb from limb, but what else could I have done?"

"I think you were very clever," Cillay said around the ache in her throat.

"Yes, I thought so, too. Hold it, stop digging."

Cillay froze. "Are they coming?"

"No. The fat one is standing on the steps, looking this way. Be still until she goes in again."

They waited for several minutes, and then they distinctly heard the back door slam.

218

"She's gone. Go on, or do you want me to take a turn?"

"No. I'm all right." She continued to stab angrily at the dirt, breaking off disappointingly small pieces which were then removed with the shovel. At this rate by dark they'd only be able to get a hand or a foot through the hole, not an entire body. And so far no one had come along the alley at all. She told herself that the tears running freely down her cheeks were despair over their predicament, but she knew it wasn't true. She had let herself care too much about Sam Chellmand, and she ought to have known better.

She stabbed and dug until her hands were full of blisters, then took a turn at the window while Mrs. Sanding dug, then went back until her blisters broke. Grimly, she wrapped the bleeding hands with the stockings that had been used for gags, and continued to dig.

It was far into the afternoon, and they'd passed the point where they discussed their hunger and what they'd like to eat if it were available, when Alan suddenly moved and tried to sit up.

Cillay dropped the pick and ran eagerly to his side. "Alan? Alan, are you better?"

For a moment his eyes were glazed; then, gradually, they seemed to clear and focus upon her face.

"Cillay?"

"Yes. Don't worry, we're trying to dig our way out, only the ground is so hard . . . but we have until dark, at least. I'm sure we'll make it."

"Cillay . . ." he sounded dazed and sank back against the sacking on which he lay. "Got to tell

219

. . . Sam. He was right . . . I should have left it alone . . ."

"Alan . . . why were you here? What were you looking for?"

He mumbled something incoherent and seemed to sink back into a stupor.

Cillay and Mrs. Sanding regarded one another with concern. "He ought to have medical attention, and water to drink. The least they could do would be to give us some water."

"They think we're too tied up to be able to drink," Mrs. Sanding reminded her. "Let me see if I can find something else to dig with . . . I think we're going to have to risk working at the same time without a guard, or we'll never make it."

They continued to chisel away, both of them with bleeding hands now, neither of them having any particular sense of humor left. And then, when the hole had gotten large enough to get a head through, they began to tunnel under the wall of the garage. And came to an abrupt halt.

Cillay stopped with a cry, appalled when the edge of the shovel touched a surface that was quite immovable.

"What is it? What's the matter?"

She put her fingers into the hole and touched the smooth surface of a concrete pipe.

"It's a sewer pipe or something. A big one, look."

In the four inch section exposed there was little curvature. Mrs. Sanding touched it, too, her shoulders sagging wearily. "I'll say it's a big one. We haven't got a chance of digging under it. Unless they leave us here until early in the morning."

Cillay was near tears, but she didn't want to show them. She sat down on one of the lumpy sacks and surveyed her hands.

"I don't think we're going to get out of here. Maybe we'd better break a window and start screaming, even if we don't see anyone."

"That's a last resort, you know. If Beatrice hears us before the neighbors do, they won't leave us in any condition to get loose and yell another time."

"No. I suppose not. I'm so hungry! I wonder what's in these sacks?" She bent over to inspect the label more closely. "Grass seed. Whatever do you suppose anyone wanted with fifty pounds of grass seed, on a lot that is ninety-five per cent covered with house?"

"Is grass seed edible?" Mrs. Sanding wondered. "Try it and see."

Cillay stood up and opened the sack, which was not sealed. "Doesn't look like much, but I suppose . . ." Her voice trailed off as her fingers encountered some foreign material in the tiny seeds. She drew out what she had touched and stared at it.

Mrs. Sanding rose in alarm when Cillay began to laugh, for the laughter was tinged with hysteria. Cillay shook her head, holding out what she had found.

"They're going crazy, tearing the house apart for this, and it's here! It's right here with us!"

"Hundred dollar bills. How many are there?"

Cillay dug her hands deeply into the seeds. "I think it's only seeds on the very top! Here, feel! What a place to hide a fortune! I wonder why it was hidden here? I guess we'll never know about that, now. Can't you see Beatrice getting blacker in the face because they can't find it?"

221

The old lady handed the money back to her. "Cover it up again. It can't do us any good unless we get out of here, and I, for one, would rather see it stay there until it rots than turn it over to those two."

And so they buried the money and rested and wondered what, other than waylaying Beatrice and Pet when they returned, they could do to escape.

They watched in vain for anyone moving in the alleyway. "Thursday mornings," Mrs. Sanding said, "that's when the garbage men come. Apparently no one else uses the alley."

"Thursday. That's two days away. That's too late to do us any good."

"Yes. All we can do is be ready for them when they come back."

When lights came on in the house next door they finally decided to break the window, knowing that Beatrice would be as likely to hear them as the neighbors would. Cillay did it with the pry bar, making a terrible racket, while Mrs. Sanding watched the house.

"No one coming out," she reported. "Stick your head out and yell."

Cillay could not put her head through the opening, but she pressed her face to it, careful of the shards of glass remaining, and shouted as loudly as she could for help.

There was no response whatever from the house across the way.

"They're playing a radio," she said. "Quite loudly. They can't hear me."

Night fell and it grew cold. No more balmy September evenings; this was going to be the forerunner of winter, Cillay thought. The air smelled of frost. Oc-

222

casionally Alan moaned and stirred in his unnatural sleep. They wrapped the single blanket tightly around him (neither of them mentioned the bedspread wrapped around the motionless form just inside the doors) and found a few empty gunny sacks to add to the blanket. There was nothing else they could do for him, and in a way Cillay was glad that he continued to sleep, although she knew it was not a good sign.

They had taken up places on either side of the doors, keeping their weapons ready. For a long time they waited, growing stiffer and colder, thinking of warm beds and hot food and water to drink.

Cillay thought, too, of Sam. Who lived with Mrs. Chellmand (were there any little Chellmands? Mrs. Sanding had neglected to say) in a lovely home, a safe, warm place. *You shouldn't have let me begin to care about you, Sam,* she told him silently, reproachfully. *It wasn't fair of you.*

Once in a while one of them went to the window to look out. There were still lights on in the back part of the house. Presumably someone had fed the remaining boarders and was now washing up. What excuse had they made for the continued disappearances? Did Miss Appleton and Mr. Gary believe them? Not that it made any difference, for they were destined for the same fate as the others. A fiery pyre. Would the garage go, too, and the bag of currency with it? Cillay wondered listlessly. There would be a certain justice in that, only it was too bad that Beatrice and "Pet" could not know.

The lights in the back of the house went out, and still no one came. Cillay flexed her tightening shoulder muscles. How much damage could she inflict with that baby sledge hammer? Any time before today she would also have been wondering if she would have the nerve to strike anyone with such a weapon, but tonight she had no doubts on that score. When Beatrice came through the door that hammer would descend on her, full force.

Although it brought immediately jumping nerves, it was a relief when they finally heard footsteps outside, and someone began to fumble with the padlock. Neither of them breathing audibly, they rose, hands tightening painfully around the handles of the sledge hammer and the pruning shears. And when the door finally opened and a figure moved through the narrow passageway, both of them brought their weapons down as hard as they could.

The grunt of pain that followed was a distinctly masculine one, as was the voice that demanded, "What the hell . . . ?"

A flashlight came on, and the sledge hammer slid from her fingers onto her own big toe as Cillay stared in dismay at their victim.

"Oh, good heavens," said Mrs. Sanding. "It's that poor Mr. Chellmand."

Chapter 21

"Or what's left of him," Sam said irritably. "I think you've broken my shoulder, and something stabbed me in the ribs . . . You've ripped one of my best suits."

"Well, we weren't expecting *you*," Cillay apologized.

"What are you doing burgling in your best suit?" Mrs. Sanding asked reasonably.

"I didn't know you'd be so particular about what I wore, or I'd have taken time to go home and change. As it was, I came straight from the airport, and I thought I was doing you a favor." He still sounded disgruntled, and he was massaging the injured shoulder as if it were extremely tender.

"You have. We couldn't unlock the door, and we tried to tunnel out but there's a sewer pipe or something the full length of that side of the garage . . ."

"There's a badly injured boy here," Mrs. Sanding interjected, "and he needs an ambulance. We can discuss everything else later."

"There's an ambulance on the way. Also the police," Sam said succinctly. "I hadn't expected to be one of the patients, however."

"We're sorry . . ." Cillay stretched out a hand, palm up, in a placating gesture, and Sam immediately took it.

"My God," he said contritely, "here I am complaining about a little sledge hammer and a butcher knife,

225

or whatever you stuck me with, and you've all got to be taken to the hospital. Who's hurt . . . Alan?"

"Yes. There's a wicked looking slash on his head, and he's only been semi-conscious for a few minutes at a time."

"Aren't you going to say *I told you so?*" Sam asked, releasing her hand. "Damn it, I was sure he'd gone home, the way I told him to."

"Who is he? What was he doing here?" Cillay demanded.

Sam had walked past them to bend over the boy, examining him by the light of the flash. "His name is Alan Creighton Armstrong. His father's a well-to-do business man here in town. He got the idea he would be able to find out what was going on in this house if he came to live here."

"And what was going on?" Mrs. Sanding wanted to know. "What connection does he have with it?"

"His uncle lived here for a short time. A Mr. James Armstrong. An elderly and reputedly wealthy eccentric. He died within a week of coming to this house to live . . . oh, nothing wrong with that, he had a stroke and was taken to the hospital and didn't survive, which was not too unexpected as he was seventy-five and had had two strokes previously. However, when his family came for his things they found he didn't have anything of value. Nothing at all. Even his bank account had been depleted, and he'd been known to have a collection of diamond rings and valuable tie pins, that sort of thing. Mrs. Pomeroy insisted he hadn't had anything like that, so far as she knew."

He touched Alan gently and stood up.

"But there'll be other people needing you, too," Sam said, very gently.

"There's no one . . . no one but Pam."

"There will be," Sam insisted. "You'll want a home of your own some day. A husband and a family."

I thought of that, she told him silently, *before I found out you were married.*

Their journey was suddenly over. Sam drove through a gateway in a high brick wall, into grounds that were now dark, but she could see a lighted house through the trees. A large, elegant house, with warm lights spilling out across the lawn, welcomingly.

The motor died when he turned off the ignition and for a moment they sat, looking out at the house.

"This is where I've lived since I was born," Sam told her. "Do you like it?"

She could not speak, and she could not stop the tears. Sam leaned toward her, with that familiar scent about him, his face concerned.

"What's the matter? Cillay, darling, it's all over . . . don't worry about any of it any more, let me take care of everything. I want to take care of you . . . I almost died, thinking what might be happening to you, while I was flying back here . . . Can't you imagine what it was like, thinking maybe that ambulance would be needed for you?"

"How . . . how can you . . ." she choked, and then broke off. For the front door had opened and a woman stood there in the lighted doorway.

Sam reached across her and opened the car door, nudging her out ahead of him. She moved numbly, wishing she wouldn't make such a poor showing,

Pam, and he said they'll have a vacancy soon, they could probably take her."

Cillay jerked herself upright. "Oh, no, you leave her alone! I promised my mother she'd never go into one of those places . . ."

"One of what places? Do you have any idea of the sort of place I'm talking about? Your sister is retarded, yes, but she's quite capable of taking simple orders, of learning to do simple things . . . There's a good chance she could learn to do something that would make her self-supporting."

"She doesn't need to be self-supporting. If Aunt Elsa's money comes to me there'll be enough for me to take care of her." Her lips were trembling and her throat ached so that she could scarcely speak.

"But that may not be what's best for Pam, darling. Have you thought of that? This school is a marvelous place, they do wonders for children like Pam."

Darling. He had called her darling. In the darkened car the tears spilled over and ran down her cheeks.

"I won't put her in an institution."

"This isn't an institution. At least not like the ones you're thinking of. It's a lovely place. I'll take you to see it, and to talk to Dr. Maynes, and you'll see for yourself. There's nothing to be afraid of. And Pam might like it there very much . . . she'd be with other children like herself. Have you ever thought how lonely it must be, to be like Pam and moving always among normal people?"

She managed to swallow her sob before she answered. "Pam has me. That's all she needs." *And what about me,* she wondered guiltily. *Is Pam all I need?*

233

called home, too," Sam told her. "She's probably been put to bed by this time, and that's what we'll do with you, once we've got your poor hands taken care of."

"Go along, dear, I'm sure Mr. Chellmand will take good care of you," Mrs. Sanding assured her. "We'll get your money inside and see that the house is locked up . . . although we're probably perfectly safe now, with those two gone!"

Cillay wanted to call after them, to ask Mrs. Sanding to go with them to get Pam and bring her back, but she couldn't bring out the words and Sam's touch was about to reduce her to tears.

"I can't go anywhere looking like this," she managed finally, looking down at her dirtied sweater and slacks.

"Don't be an idiot. Who expects you to look like a model after what you've been through? Come on, they're expecting us."

He had driven his own car from the airport, and he handed her into it and slid in beside her. Cillay huddled in her own corner, wondering if it wouldn't have been easier, after all, to have allowed Beatrice to finish her off, than to go home with Sam to meet his charming wife.

"I've been thinking about your sister," he said as they eased out into the street. "Has she ever gone to school?"

"No." Her voice was stiff, reserved. "She . . . can't ever compete with normal children. Not even with very young children."

"No, I meant a special school for retarded children. I know a doctor who operates a place for retarded children, right here in the city. I talked to him about eaten since yesterday. I don't suppose there's a steak in the house, but maybe there's some soup in the cupboard."

They moved toward the kitchen, but Sam, still talking rapidly on the telephone, reached out a hand to catch Cillay's wrist.

"All right. We'll be along directly," he said into the receiver, and hung it up. "Look, you people, the police will be asking questions of all of you tomorrow, I'm sure, but you're probably safe to go to bed now. Only I'm taking Cillay along with me . . . she's had a rough time, and I want a doctor to look at her hands . . ."

Cillay made a protesting movement. "No. The house is my responsibility now. At least I think it is. Aunt Elsa wrote my mother that she was leaving everything to me . . . oh!"

Mrs. Sanding had stopped, too, her eyes widening. "Good heavens, we forgot about the money! There's a whole feed sack full of money out there in the garage! Someone ought to bring it inside, I suppose," she said, and giggled girlishly.

"Come along and show me," Mr. Gary offered, "and I'll be happy to oblige."

"Fine. Meanwhile, I'm taking Cillay home with me . . ."

"No. I'll come back here. I only want to get my sister." Her voice and her face were stiff. She wouldn't ask anything of this lovely, generous wife of Sam's; she didn't even want to meet her, and she wished he would stop holding her wrist so possessively, as if he had a right to hold it.

"Your sister is perfectly happy where she is. I

231

wishing she had had the strength to stand up to him and not come, wishing she were dead.

"Sam . . . I've been so worried! Is everything all right?"

"Yes, everything's fine! We'll tell you about it later . . . right now this girl needs a warm bath and possibly a doctor to look at her hands, or maybe you can fix them up. And something to eat. She hasn't eaten since last night."

"Oh, you poor child! Come on in! Your sister is still up; she's playing with the piano . . . She's quite fascinated with it, I wonder if she couldn't be taught to play it?"

Through blurred eyes Cillay made out the woman who had come to welcome her into the hallway. A tall, white-haired woman in a blue dress, a kindly face . . . a face much like Sam's. *Mrs. Chellmand?*

Behind her, his hand firm on her arm, Sam spoke. "Mother, this is Cillay."

"Such a lovely name," Mrs. Chellmand said. "And a lovely girl . . . I always knew Sam would choose a lovely girl. Come in, Cillay, and we'll get you a bath first . . . or are you more hungry than dirty?"

Sam would choose a lovely girl . . . She was stunned, bemused, and not by the perfection of the house they had entered. This woman was not Sam's wife, but his mother. And she had said Sam would choose a lovely girl . . .

"Go along with her, darling," Sam said, releasing her reluctantly. "I'll check on Pam, and we'll have a snack with you when you come down. Be careful with her, Mother, she's been through a lot today."

"But she's made of rather tough stuff, I suspect," Mrs. Chellmand observed. "I don't suppose you've had time to make any plans . . ."

Cillay was staring at her blankly.

"I understand you're new in the city, and have no family except your sister. So you'll no doubt want a quiet wedding . . . I'll be happy to do all the things your own mother would do, if she were here, my dear."

Wedding . . . her lips formed the word, but no sound came. Sam took an impatient step after them.

"Damn it, the least you could do is let me do my own proposing," he said.

Mrs. Chellmand's eyebrows rose gracefully. "You mean you haven't . . . ? Well, I'm sorry, my dear, but when you called to tell me you were bringing home your future wife, that you've finally found *the* girl, I naturally assumed you'd asked how *she* felt about it!"

"We only met a few days ago, and you can't expect a girl to make up her mind all that fast, just because I did," Sam pointed out.

"Of course not," Mrs. Chellmand agreed. "Well, you can propose in your own good time, but right now we'll get this girl a bath and a change of clothes, if you can bring yourself to let go of her again."

Cillay felt her hand slide away from his (for he had momentarily recaptured it, carefully so as not to hurt her), and the warmth and happiness that flooded her were such as she had never known. Sam was watching her, somewhat apprehensively, for he had not planned it this way.

Cillay's eyes met his, still brimming, but with a happy message. She couldn't tell if he read it correctly, but her wavering smile brought forth one from him in return, and then she broke away and went with his mother up the wide, curving stairway.

Mrs. Chellmand led her into a large bedroom, exquisitely decorated in pale pinks with a touch of wine red, and through it into a tiled and mirrored bath. "There are towels, and I've laid out a dressing gown . . . That will do for tonight and in the morning we'll see about getting your own clothes here, or some new ones . . ." She lingered, her smile deepening. "Sam is my only son, you know, and I love him dearly. But he is rather stupid in some ways . . . We'll talk again, about the wedding."

"Yes," Cillay agreed, her smile breaking freely forth. "We will. But don't tell Sam yet."

"Never a word," Mrs. Chellmand agreed, and they stood there, grinning at one another rather foolishly for a moment.

And then Sam's mother was gone, and she was alone. But not really alone, she thought, her spirits rising. With Sam downstairs, she would never be alone again. She turned on the water in the big white tub and began to undress, moving slowly, no longer tired or even hungry.

But in a little while she would begin to hurry again, to dress and go down those wide, curving stairs. Because Sam was down there. Waiting for her.

LOOK FOR OUR MAGNUM CLASSICS

CARNIVAL OF DEATH

They moved along the Midway, Cillay and Sam, Pam and Alan, pausing to watch a shooting contest at one of the booths. Pam wasn't interested in the shooting: only in the prizes. She set her eye on a big pink teddy bear.

"Go ahead," said Sam, amused. "Win it for her, Alan. You can shoot, can't you?"

"I can shoot," said Alan, grimly. He dug a half dollar from his pocket, and accepted the rifle.

Cillay watched, relaxed. She felt happy for the first time in many months—she had needed this badly, this evening out with young people, laughing, talking . . .

There was shooting going on all around them, for there were booths on the other side of the Midway, too—so much shooting that no one noticed an extra shot, one not intended for a metal target.

No one saw who fired the gun at Cillay. But she felt the burning sensation, and collapsed into Sam's arms . . .

PUT PLEASURE IN YOUR READING
Larger type makes the difference
This EASY EYE Edition is set in large, clear type—at least 30 percent larger than usual. It is printed on scientifically tinted non-glare paper for better contrast and less eyestrain.